Retelling Tales with HEADBANDS

Editorial Development: Joy Evans
                       De Gibbs
                       Camille Liscinsky
Copy Editing: Cathy Harber
Art Direction: Cheryl Puckett
Cover Design: Liliana Potigian
Illustration: Shirley Beckes
              Jo Larsen
Design/Production: Olivia C. Trinidad
                   John D. Williams

EMC 3322

Evan-Moor
EDUCATIONAL PUBLISHERS
Helping Children Learn since 1979

**Congratulations on your
purchase of some of the
finest teaching materials
in the world.**

**Correlated
to State Standards**

For information about other Evan-Moor products, call 1-800-777-4362,
fax 1-800-777-4332, or visit our Web site, www.evan-moor.com.
Entire contents © 2009 EVAN-MOOR CORP.
18 Lower Ragsdale Drive, Monterey, CA 93940-5746. Printed in USA.

Visit *teaching-standards.com* to view a
correlation of this book's activities to your
state's standards. This is a free service.

Contents

What's Inside

Dramatic play is a proven way to effectively build reading fluency and comprehension. Retelling favorite and familiar tales is a form of dramatic play that is particularly well-suited to early and emergent readers. The practice of sharing tales with children promotes literary response and analysis. Teaching children to retell the tales helps them develop a variety of critical listening, speaking, and comprehension skills.

Retelling Tales with Headbands provides the following materials for classroom dramatic play that is meaningful, engaging, and FUN!

- 10 age- and length-appropriate versions of familiar fables, fairy tales, and folk tales

- suggestions for sharing the tales with children and guiding them through the retelling process

- 2 to 6 reproducible headband patterns for each tale

- 3 reproducible activities per tale to support comprehension and give students extra practice in character recognition, sequencing, and literary response

Each unit in this book includes:

Teaching Guidelines

Teaching suggestions for each tale are presented in ten easy-to-follow steps. The first six steps focus on comprehension and literary analysis. The next four steps set the stage for dramatic play and prepare students to retell the story in their own words.

Story Text

Each tale has been rewritten in simple but exciting prose, incorporating repetition, rhyme, and appropriate vocabulary in short, easy-to-follow paragraphs. Each tale also features five drawings that illustrate the story's main events.

Character Recognition Activities

One page of reproducible activities features pictures of the story's characters with their names printed in traceable letters or as part of a matching exercise. One or two simple questions follow to further support character recognition and identification.

Sequencing Practice

A second reproducible page contains the story's five illustrations, repeated as blackline drawings for the students to color. The pictures are numbered sequentially to follow the story and can be used in a variety of ways to help students remember the order of events and to reinforce the concepts of beginning, middle, and end.

Follow-up Activities

A third reproducible activity page is designed to provide practice in listening and following simple directions to identify characters, trace letters, draw, and color.

Headband Patterns

Reproducible patterns for each story's characters are included for students to color, cut out, and assemble into headbands. The headbands can be used in both sharing and retelling activities.

Skills and Standards

The activities presented in this book correlate with the following language arts content standards for early learners:

- retelling a familiar tale

- understanding main events

- sequencing events in a story

- identifying characters, setting, and supporting details

- making predictions

- comparing and contrasting

- listening attentively

- following simple directions

How to Use the Book

Before children can successfully retell a story, they must understand the story. Discussing its parts, particularly its characters, setting, and sequence of events, is an important aid to comprehension. Providing related background information further promotes understanding and often has the added advantage of supporting other academic areas, such as science, social studies, or math.

The teaching suggestions in this book offer a step-by-step approach to introducing stories, helping students understand them, and engaging students in retelling practice, performance, and related activities.

1 Build Background

Use the specific, age-appropriate suggestions provided to help introduce content, characters, and setting. Reproduce "Meet the Characters" pages to actively involve students in this important first step.

2 Read the Story

The suggestions included for this step are designed to help you gain and hold students' attention as you read the story aloud. They are intended to draw the students directly into the reading. Echoing or chanting words, sounds, rhymes, or refrains can help early learners develop listening, fluency, and phonemic awareness skills.

3 Reread the Story

To retell a story, students typically need to hear the story at least three or four times. Repeated readings aid comprehension and provide multiple opportunities to model oral fluency. Use the reproducible "Follow the Story" page in each unit to help keep students engaged through multiple readings. They can use the sequentially numbered illustrations on the page to follow along during the readings, either independently or as directed.

4 Talk About the Story

After reading and rereading the story, ask the students to imagine themselves as the characters and talk about how the characters would act. Using the "Follow the Story" page during the discussion will help reinforce both comprehension and sequencing.

5 Make Headbands

Headbands are a fun and easy alternative to costumes for dramatic play. Making the headbands as a class project engages students in hands-on activity that helps develop fine motor skills and, at the same time, supports character recognition. The instructions for assembling the headbands in this book are conveniently described and illustrated on the reproducible pattern pages. This activity also requires crayons, scissors, and a stapler.

6 Read Other Versions

Most fables, folk tales, and fairy tales are centuries old, and retelling them over time has resulted in any number of variations. Reading some of the variations and then asking students to point out similarities and differences is an effective way to practice comparing and contrasting.

7 Assign Roles and Practice Actions

For the most part, you will assign roles to your students as you see fit, but specific suggestions are also provided to help you match students' skills and personalities to certain characters. After assigning roles, defining and practicing story-related actions are necessary steps for students to understand the characters in the context of the story. Practice also improves comprehension and fluency and helps build confidence and self-esteem.

8 Set Up Scenery and Props

The staging suggestions in each unit are intentionally limited to keep the focus of activities on building comprehension and oral language skills, particularly fluency. Because the stories are familiar tales, the headbands and a few simple props are all you need for the students or an audience to recognize the characters and setting and to follow the story.

9 Retell the Story

The ultimate goal of steps 1 through 8 is preparing students to retell a story fluently and in their own words. Besides the obvious language arts benefits of retelling activities, this type of group dramatic play also helps students develop social skills and promotes cooperation and respect for others.

10 Invite an Audience

To further reinforce reading and fluency skills and to provide support and recognition from outside the classroom, you may want to have your students retell their stories in front of an audience. A reproducible invitation is included at the back of the book (page 176) to help you "take the show on the road."

The Lion and the Mouse

*Little Mouse's size doesn't keep him
from helping a mighty Lion.*

Handouts

*Reproduce for each
student.*

- Meet the
  Characters
  Page 13

- Follow the Story
  Page 14

Headbands

*Make a headband
pattern for each
student.*

- Lion
  Pages 16 and 17

- Mouse
  Pages 18 and 19

① Build Background

Distribute page 13 and tell students they will be hearing a make-believe
story about a lion and a mouse who meet in a jungle. Have students point
to each character on the page as you read its name. Share some relevant
facts about the characters, such as that a mouse has sharp teeth that can
nibble through wood and rope, and a lion has sharp claws for grabbing
and holding things.

Guide students through the activities on the page. Then have them pose
as lions and roar loudly and then pose as mice and squeak quietly. Ask for
a show of hands as to which of the two animals is scarier.

② Read *The Lion and the Mouse*

Read the story aloud. Show students the illustrations as you read. Use a
deep, powerful voice for the lion and a squeaky, timid voice for the mouse.

③ Reread the Story

Distribute page 14. Tell students to look at the pictures on the page as you
reread the story. The pictures are arranged and numbered in story sequence.
When you come to an illustration in the story, have the students find the
picture on the sheet that shows what you are reading about. Ask them to
point to the picture. You may also want to ask them to tell you the number
of the picture. Explain how the numbers can help them follow the story.

④ Talk About the Story

Have the students color the pictures on page 14. Encourage them to talk
about what's happening in the pictures as they work.

⑤ Make Headbands

Give each student a headband pattern to color, cut out, and assemble.
You may want to have the students work in groups, with each group
making headbands for a particular character. Invite students to wear
their headbands as you read the story again. Encourage them to
pantomime the actions of their headband's character.

⑥ Read Other Versions

Gather other versions of *The Lion and the Mouse* to read to the students,
and then lead them in comparing and contrasting the different versions.

7 Assign Roles and Practice Actions

Assign the role of the lion to students who are particularly exuberant and energetic. Students who tend to be reserved may be more comfortable playing the mouse.

Have students look at their "Follow the Story" pictures as you review the tale's main events with them. Invite students to suggest ways to act out these events. Then give them time to practice their actions.

8 Set Up Scenery and Props

To create a simple jungle setting, you could draw trees on the board or hang long strips of green crepe paper from the ceiling. To simulate a net, loosely drape yarn, string, or a blanket over the lion character.

9 Retell the Story

Have students wear their headbands and retell the story in their own words. For each pair of storytellers, introduce the story and its setting as a signal to begin.

10 Invite an Audience *(optional)*

When the students are comfortable retelling the story, you may want to invite an audience to watch them and cheer them on. You will find a reproducible invitation on page 176.

Props
• Yarn, string, or blanket

After the Story
Reproduce page 15 for each student. Distribute the copies and help students complete the activities.

The Lion and the Mouse

One hot summer day, Lion was asleep in the shade. It was too hot to run. It was too hot to pounce. It was even too hot to roar.

But it was not too hot for little Mouse. He was hungry. Mouse was so hungry that he did not look where he was going. Mouse ran right on top of Lion. His tiny claws went *scritch, scritch, scratch* across Lion's nose!

EMC 3322 • © Evan-Moor Corp.

With lightning speed, Lion grabbed Mouse by the tail.

"You look like a tasty snack," said Lion. And he opened his great big mouth.

Mouse began to squeak. "Please don't hurt me, Mr. Lion. Please let me go. Maybe I can help you someday."

Lion looked at the tiny mouse and began to laugh. "I am the king of the jungle. I am big and strong. You're too small to help me. But you have made me laugh, so I am going to let you go."

Lion opened his big paw, and Mouse scurried away.

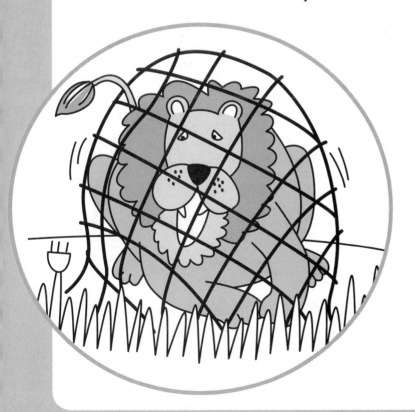

Not long after, Lion was walking through the grass when, suddenly, he stepped into a trap. He was caught in a big net. Lion pulled and tugged at the net, but he could not get free. Lion roared and roared. His roars made the grass shake and the leaves shiver.

Can you guess who heard Lion roar?

Yes, Mouse!

Mouse hurried to the lion.

"Mr. Lion, do you remember me? I can help you," said Mouse.

Mouse nibbled and nibbled on the net. And then, he nibbled some more. Mouse nibbled until the net had a big hole in it. The hole was just the right size for Lion to crawl through. Lion was free!

"Thank you, Mouse," said Lion. "You may be little, but you have a big, kind heart."

Name _____

Meet the Characters

Trace the names.

lion

mouse

Match the picture and the name.

• mouse

• lion

Read and circle the answer.

I am big.

I am little.

Name _____

Follow the Story

The Lion and
the Mouse

1

2

3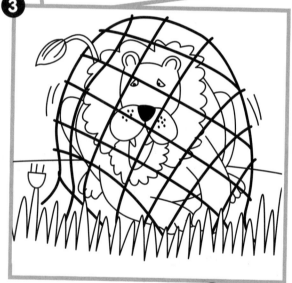

4

5

EMC 3322 • © Evan-Moor Corp.

Name _____

After the Story

Trace the sentence. Circle who said it.

The Lion and the Mouse

I can help you.

Listen and follow the directions.

1. Draw a net on Lion.

2. Color the picture.

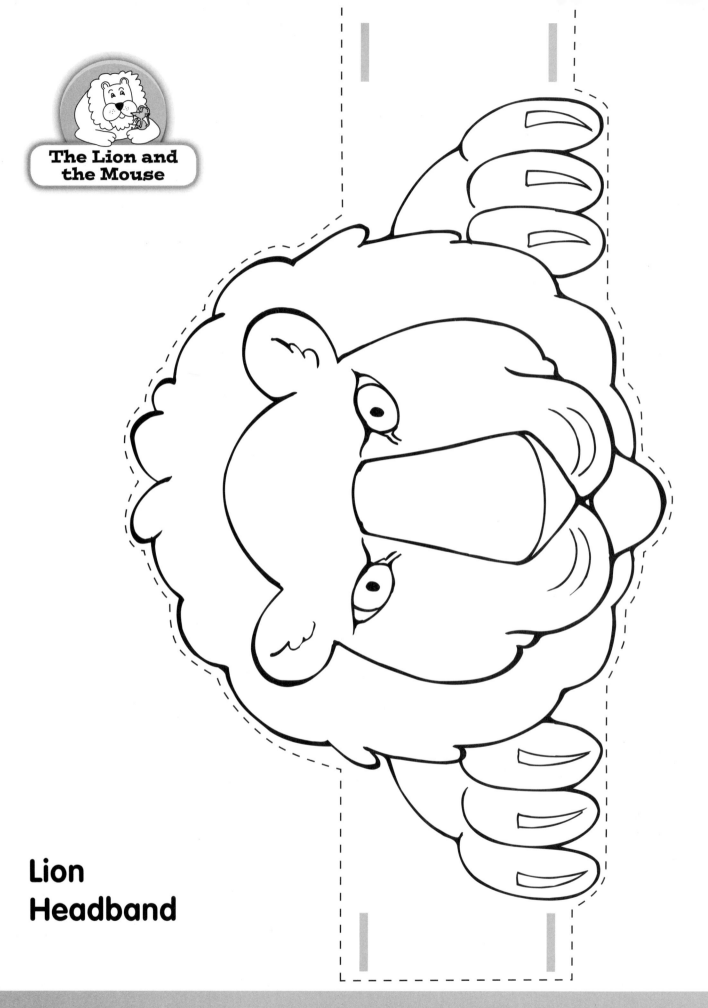

Lion
Headband

1. Cut out the three pieces of the headband.
   Cut along the dashed lines.

2. Staple the pieces together.

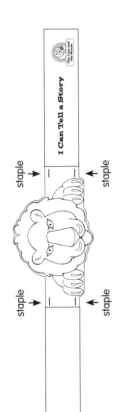

staple → ← staple

staple → ← staple

I Can Tell a Story

3. Fit the band around the student's head and staple the ends together.

I Can Tell a Story

The Lion and the Mouse

The Lion and the Mouse

Mouse
Headband

1 Cut out the three pieces of the headband. Cut along the dashed lines.

2 Staple the pieces together.

3 Fit the band around the student's head and staple the ends together.

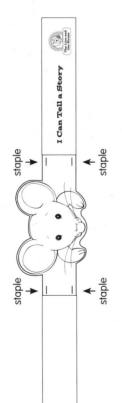

I Can Tell a Story

staple →

← staple

staple →

← staple

I Can Tell a Story

The Lion and the Mouse

Cowboy Hats for Sale

Mischievous monkeys can't resist playing "Monkey See, Monkey Do" with a cowboy's hats.

Handouts

Reproduce for each student.

- Meet the Characters
  Page 25
- Follow the Story
  Page 26

Headbands

Make a headband pattern for each student.

- Hat
  Pages 28 and 29
- Monkey
  Pages 30 and 31

1 Build Background

Distribute page 25 and tell students they will be hearing a make-believe story about a cowboy who sells cowboy hats and meets a group of playful monkeys. Share some relevant facts about the characters, such as that a cowboy wears a cowboy hat to keep the sun out of his eyes and the rain off his face, and that monkeys can grab things with their hands, and they often imitate, or copy, the actions they see people do.

Guide students through the activities on the page. Then invite them to play "Monkey See, Monkey Do." Have the students pretend to be monkeys, with one being the leader. As in "Simon Says," the monkeys follow the leader's commands to do simple actions, but only if the leader starts the command with "Monkey says...."

2 Read *Cowboy Hats for Sale*

Read the story aloud. Show students the illustrations as you read. Invite students to make the monkey sounds whenever they come up in the story.

3 Reread the Story

Distribute page 26. Tell students to look at the pictures on the page as you reread the story. The pictures are arranged and numbered in story sequence. When you come to an illustration in the story, have the students find the picture on the sheet that shows what you are reading about. Ask them to point to the picture. You may also want to ask them to tell you the number of the picture. Explain how the numbers can help them follow the story.

4 Talk About the Story

Have the students color the pictures on page 26. Encourage them to talk about what's happening in the pictures as they work.

5 Make Headbands

Give each student a headband pattern to color, cut out, and assemble. You may want to have the students work in groups, with one group making hat headbands and the other group making monkey headbands. Make enough hats so each monkey can be wearing one when the cowboy wakes up. Invite students to wear their headbands as you read the story again. Encourage them to pantomime the actions of their headband's character.

6 Read Other Versions

Cowboy Hats for Sale is based on an old folk tale. Gather other versions of the folk tale to read to students, such as *Caps for Sale* and *Circus Caps for Sale,* both by Esphyr Slobodkina. Then lead the students in comparing and contrasting the different versions.

⑦ Assign Roles and Practice Actions

Assign the roles of the monkeys either to students who tend to be shy and may be hesitant to play speaking roles or to students who need an outlet for their energy. To have a girl play the main role, simply change the story to a cowgirl selling cowgirl hats.

Have students look at their "Follow the Story" pictures as you review the story's main events with them. Invite students to suggest ways to act out these events. Then give them time to practice their actions. You may also want to talk with the students about acting out events not shown in the picture sequence, such as the cowboy stomping his foot or walking down the street selling hats.

⑧ Set Up Scenery and Props

One way to make a tree for the monkeys is to draw a large tree trunk with long side branches on the board and have the monkeys stand along the branches on both sides of the tree trunk. You may want to have the cowboy or cowgirl wear a bandana or a neckerchief in addition to the hat headband.

⑨ Retell the Story

Invite students to wear their headbands and retell the story in their own words. For each group of storytellers, introduce the story and its setting as a signal to begin.

⑩ Invite an Audience *(optional)*

When students are comfortable retelling the story, you may want to invite an audience to watch them and cheer them on. You will find a reproducible invitation on page 176.

Props
- Bandana or neckerchief

After the Story
Reproduce page 27 for each student. Distribute the copies and help students complete the activities.

Cowboy Hats for Sale

Once upon a time, in an old cowboy town, there lived a cowboy who sold cowboy hats. The cowboy stacked the hats one by one on his head. First, the cowboy put on his own red cowboy hat. Next, he piled on some yellow cowboy hats. Then, he added blue hats. Finally, at the very top, he placed a white cowboy hat.

Every day, the cowboy walked up and down the dusty streets, smiling and waving to everyone. He'd say, "Howdy! Want to buy a cowboy hat?"

One sunny afternoon, the cowboy sat against a shady tree. He carefully placed the stack of cowboy hats on the grass. He left his red hat on his head and pulled it down over his eyes. He was ready for a snooze.

After a bit of snoring and dreaming, the cowboy woke up and stretched. It was time to get back to work. He pushed up his red hat from over his eyes. Then he leaped to his feet as fast as a jackrabbit. He looked to the left and then to the right. The stack of cowboy hats was gone!

The cowboy heard chattering. It was coming from high in the tree. He looked up. There, sitting on the branches, was a group of monkeys. And each monkey was wearing a cowboy hat!

The cowboy put his hands on his hips and stomped his foot. He looked up at the monkeys and shouted, "Give me back my cowboy hats!"

All the monkeys put their hands on their hips and stomped their feet. All the monkeys screeched, "Eee! Eee! Eee!"

Next, the cowboy shook his fist in the air. He yelled, "Give me back my cowboy hats!"

All the monkeys shook their fists in the air. All the monkeys screeched, "Eee! Eee! Eee!"

The monkeys did not give back the hats. So the cowboy tried being nice. He put his hands together, looked very sad, and begged, "Please, give me back my hats."

All the monkeys put their hands together, looked very sad, and screeched, "Eee! Eee! Eee!"

Finally, the cowboy gave up. "What will I do without those hats?" he worried, and he threw down his red cowboy hat onto the grass. As quick as firecrackers, all the monkeys took off their hats and threw them to the ground.

Do you know what happened next?

The cowboy put his red cowboy hat on his head and stacked all the other hats on top of it. First came the yellow cowboy hats. Then came the blue hats. Finally, on the very top, sat the white cowboy hat. The cowboy walked down the dusty street, waving and smiling to everyone. He said, "Howdy! Want to buy a cowboy hat?"

Name _____

Meet the Characters

Trace the names.

cowboy

monkey

Match the picture and the name.

• monkey

• cowboy

Read and circle the answer.

I sit in a tree.

I sell hats.

Name _____

Follow the Story

Cowboy Hats
for Sale

1

2

3

4

5

After the Story

Trace the sentence. Circle who said it.

Cowboy Hats for Sale

Howdy!

Listen and follow the directions.

1. Draw a hat on the cowboy.
2. Color the hat red.

Retelling Tales with Headbands

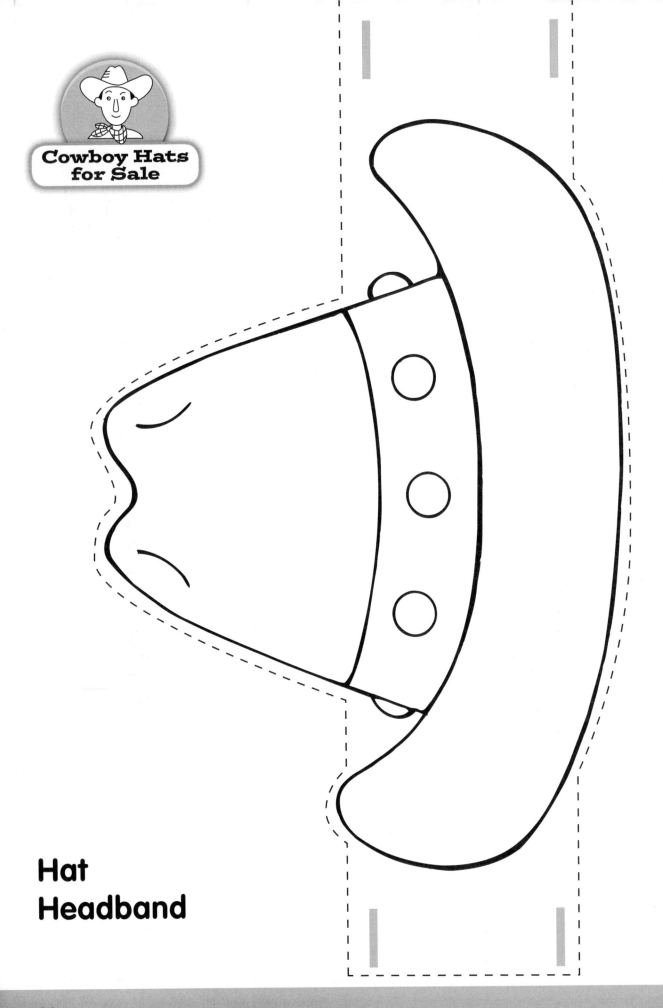

Cowboy Hats for Sale

Hat
Headband

1 Cut out the three pieces of the headband.
Cut along the dashed lines.

2 Staple the pieces together.

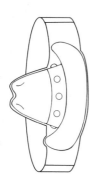

staple →

staple →

← staple

← staple

I Can Tell a Story

3 Fit the band around the student's head and staple the ends together.

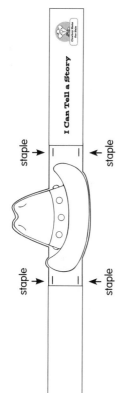

Cowboy Hats
for Sale

I Can Tell a Story

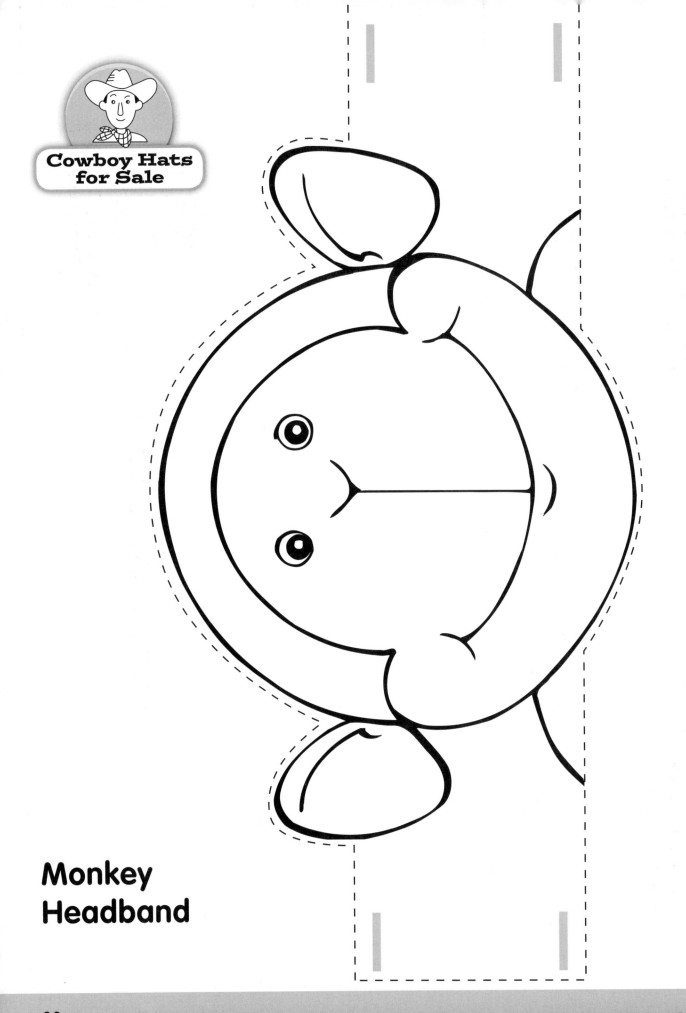

Monkey Headband

EMC 3322 • © Evan-Moor Corp.

1. Cut out the three pieces of the headband. Cut along the dashed lines.
2. Staple the pieces together.

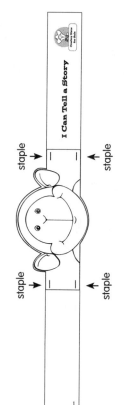

3. Fit the band around the student's head and staple the ends together.

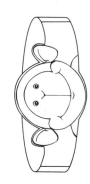

I Can Tell a Story

Cowboy Hats for Sale

The Tortoise and the Hare

A tortoise challenges a hare to a race, even though the hare has outrun every other animal.

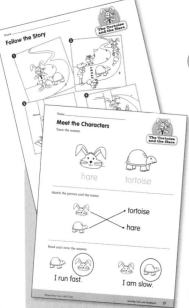

Handouts

Reproduce for each student.

- Meet the Characters
  Page 37
- Follow the Story
  Page 38

Headbands

Make a headband pattern for each student.

- Tortoise
  Pages 40 and 41
- Hare
  Pages 42 and 43
- Owl
  Pages 44 and 45

1 Build Background

Distribute page 37 and tell students they will be hearing a make-believe story about a tortoise that races a hare. Have students point to each character on the page as you read its name. Share some relevant facts about the characters, such as that a hare has big, powerful back legs that help it run very fast, while a tortoise has short, chubby legs and a heavy shell on its back, so it moves very slowly. Ask students what animal a hare looks like (a rabbit, but a hare is bigger) and what animal a tortoise looks like (a turtle, except that a turtle lives in water; a tortoise lives on land).

Guide students through the activities on the page. Then invite students to stand and move like hares and tortoises. Ask them to predict which of these two animals would most likely win a race.

2 Read *The Tortoise and the Hare*

Read the story aloud. Show students the illustrations as you read. Invite students to repeat after you the rhymes of the hare and the tortoise.

3 Reread the Story

Distribute page 38. Tell students to look at the pictures on the page as you reread the story. The pictures are arranged and numbered in story sequence. When you come to an illustration in the story, have the students find the picture on the sheet that shows what you are reading about. Ask them to point to the picture. You may also want to ask them to tell you the number of the picture. Explain how the numbers can help them follow the story.

4 Talk About the Story

Have the students color the pictures on page 38. Encourage them to talk about what's happening in the pictures as they work.

5 Make Headbands

Give each student a headband pattern to color, cut out, and assemble. You may want to have the students work in groups, with each group making headbands for a particular character. Invite students to wear their headbands as you read the story again. Encourage them to pantomime the actions of their headband's character.

6 Read Other Versions

Gather other versions of *The Tortoise and the Hare* to read to the students, and then lead them in comparing and contrasting the different versions.

⑦ Assign Roles and Practice Actions

For the roles of the tortoise and the hare, you will need students who are capable of learning the rhymes. You could also have a chorus of students say the rhymes while students portraying the tortoise and the hare pantomime the actions.

Have students look at their "Follow the Story" pictures as you review the story's main events with them. Invite students to suggest ways to act out these events. Then give them time to practice their actions.

⑧ Set Up Scenery and Props

Designate a race route through the classroom. Include "Start" and "Finish" lines made of paper and taped to the floor. For a more natural setting, consider retelling the story outdoors.

⑨ Retell the Story

Invite students to wear their headbands and retell the story in their own words. For each group of storytellers, introduce the story and its setting as a signal to begin.

⑩ Invite an Audience *(optional)*

When students are comfortable retelling the story, you may want to invite an audience to watch them and cheer them on. You will find a reproducible invitation on page 176.

Props
• Paper "Start" and "Finish" lines

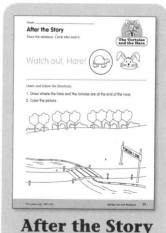

After the Story
Reproduce page 39 for each student. Distribute the copies and help students complete the activities.

The Tortoise and the Hare

Once there was a hare who ran very fast.

"I am the fastest runner in the forest!" bragged the hare. "Watch my back legs kick up the dust as I zoom along!"

The hare liked to challenge other animals to race. And the hare always won. He whooshed past the snake. He zipped past the squirrel. He even scooted past the quick red fox.

The tortoise was the only animal the hare had not raced. The tortoise carried a heavy shell on her back. She moved very slowly. One day, she was tired of hearing the hare brag. The tortoise said, "I will race you, Hare."

"You want to race me?" asked the hare. The hare puffed out his chest with pride. "Sure. Let's race. Beating you will be easy!"

The tortoise and the hare decided on the route for the race. They would run along the brook and over the bridge and end at the tree where the owl lived. The owl would be the judge.

The animals of the forest gathered on the morning of the race. The owl hooted, "Get ready. Get set. Run!"

The race began. And before you could say "Hooray!", the hare was out of sight.

The hare laughed as he ran.

I'm fast and speedy.
And you're too slow!
You'll never beat me!
Just watch me go!

The tortoise saw the hare rush off, but she did not worry.

My legs are short,
but they are strong.
I won't give up
as I move along.

The hare was tired by the time he reached the bridge. He looked back at the tortoise. All he could see was a brown dot. Feeling very confident, the hare decided to take a nap and rest his legs.

The tortoise did not give up. She was slow but steady, and as the sun began to set, the tortoise passed the hare, who was still snoozing under a tree.

The tortoise kept right on going. Slow and steady, she crossed the bridge. When she saw the finish line just ahead, the tortoise called out,

Slow and steady.
Steady and slow.
Watch out, Hare!
Here I go!

The hare woke up in a flash. He tried to hurry across the bridge, but it was too late. He saw the tortoise step over the finish line.

Owl hooted, "The tortoise is the winner! The tortoise beat the hare!" And all the animals cheered.

From that day on, the hare ran fast but he never, ever bragged again.

EMC 3322 • © Evan-Moor Corp.

Name _____

Meet the Characters

Trace the names.

hare

tortoise

Match the picture and the name.

• tortoise

• hare

Read and circle the answer.

I run fast.

I am slow.

Name _____

Follow the Story

1

2

3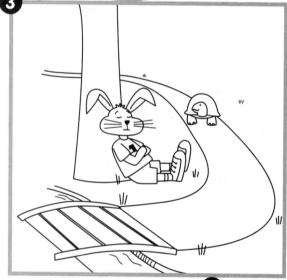

4

5

Name _____

After the Story

Trace the sentence. Circle who said it.

Watch out, Hare!

Listen and follow the directions.

1. Draw where the hare and the tortoise are at the end of the race.

2. Color the picture.

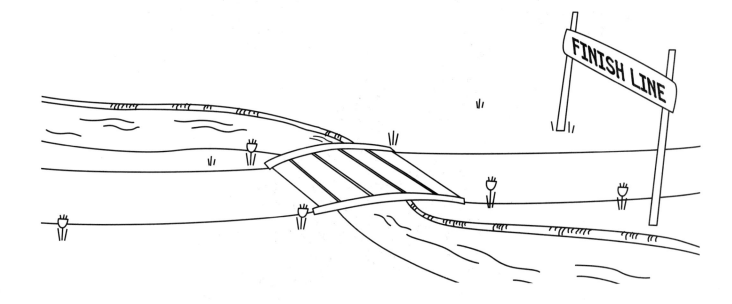

FINISH LINE

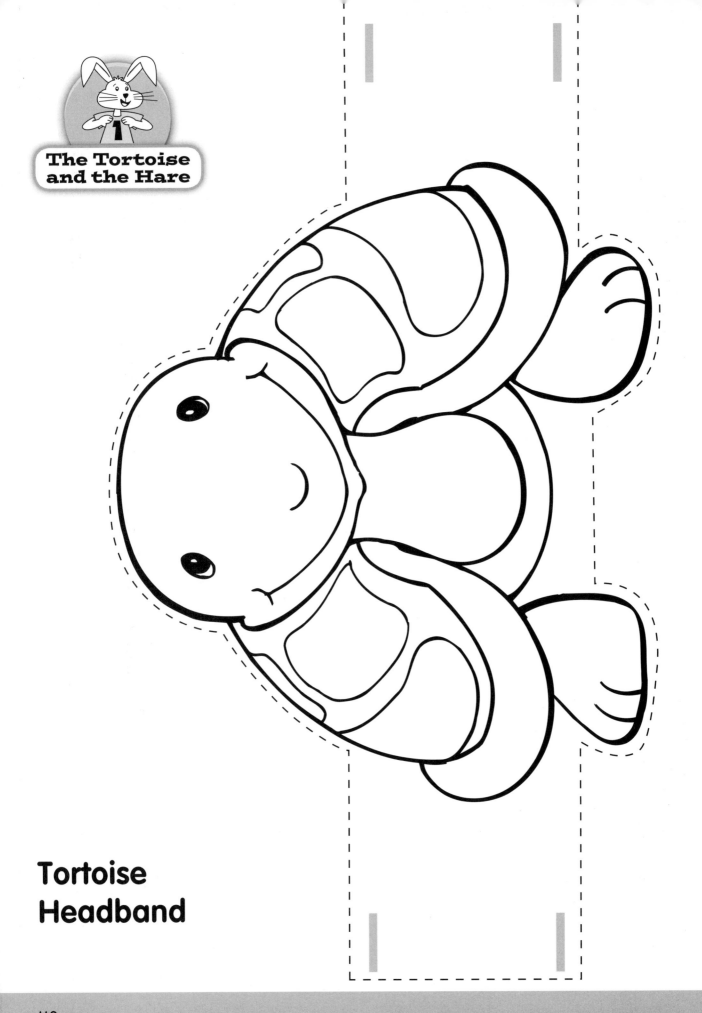

**Tortoise
Headband**

1. Cut out the three pieces of the headband.
Cut along the dashed lines.

2. Staple the pieces together.

3. Fit the band around the student's head and staple the ends together.

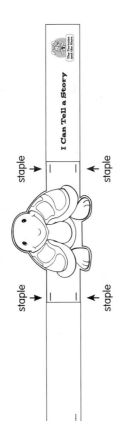

I Can Tell a Story

staple → ← staple

staple → ← staple

I Can Tell a Story

The Tortoise and the Hare

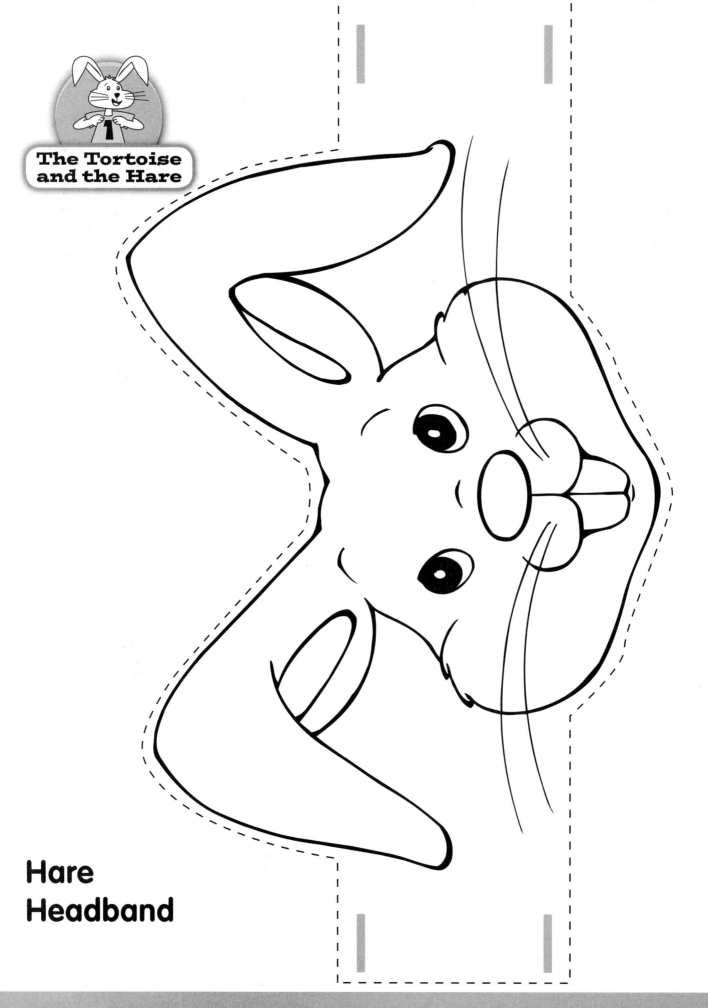

The Tortoise and the Hare

Hare
Headband

3 Fit the band around the student's head and staple the ends together.

1 Cut out the three pieces of the headband.
Cut along the dashed lines.

2 Staple the pieces together.

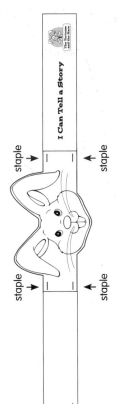

staple → ← staple

staple → ← staple

I Can Tell a Story

I Can Tell a Story

The Tortoise and the Hare

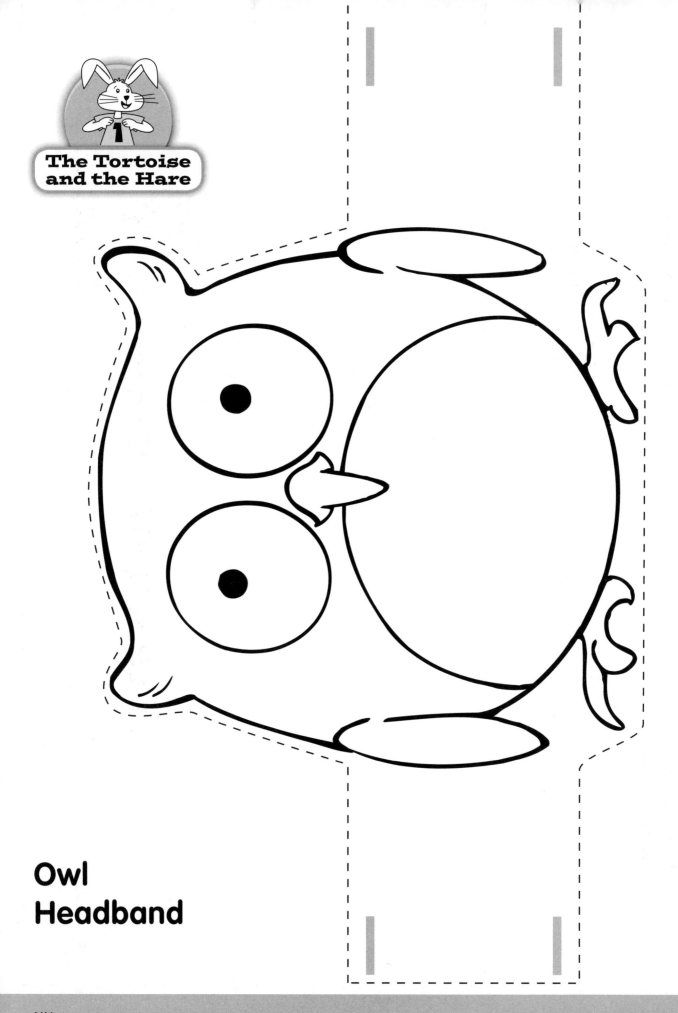

The Tortoise and the Hare

Owl
Headband

1. Cut out the three pieces of the headband.
   Cut along the dashed lines.

2. Staple the pieces together.

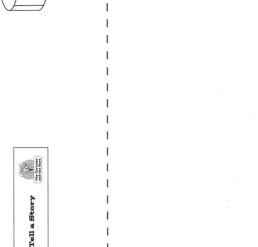

staple

staple

I Can Tell a Story

staple

staple

3. Fit the band around the student's head and staple the ends together.

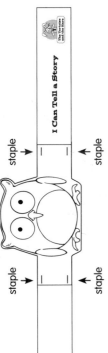

I Can Tell a Story

The Tortoise and the Hare

The Little Red Hen

Little Red Hen works hard to turn seeds into bread,
without any help from her friends.

Handouts

Reproduce for each student.

- Meet the Characters
  Page 51
- Follow the Story
  Page 52

Headbands

Make a headband pattern for each student.

- Hen
  Pages 54 and 55
- Cat
  Pages 56 and 57
- Dog
  Pages 58 and 59
- Duck
  Pages 60 and 61

1 Build Background

Distribute page 51 and tell students they will be hearing a make-believe story about a hen that asks her farmyard friends to help her grow wheat to make bread. Have students point to each character on the page as you read its name. Ask them to look closely at the pictures of the cat, dog, and duck and look for clues that predict what these animals would like to do (sleep, play, swim), instead of helping Little Red Hen.

Guide students through the activities on the page. Then share some facts about how people grow wheat and use it to make bread. Lead students in acting out the steps: planting the seeds; cutting down the stalks; threshing, or beating, the heads to separate the grain; grinding the grain into flour; using the flour to make dough; rolling and shaping the dough; and then baking it.

2 Read *The Little Red Hen*

Read the story aloud. Show students the illustrations as you read. Try using a different voice for each character and invite students to chime in each time an animal says "Not I."

3 Reread the Story

Distribute page 52. Tell students to look at the pictures on the page as you reread the story. The pictures are arranged and numbered in story sequence. When you come to an illustration in the story, have the students find the picture on the sheet that shows what you are reading about. Ask them to point to the picture. You may also want to ask them to tell you the number of the picture. Explain how the numbers can help them follow the story.

4 Talk About the Story

Have the students color the pictures on page 52. Encourage them to talk about what's happening in the pictures as they work.

5 Make Headbands

Give each student a headband pattern to color, cut out, and assemble. You may want to have the students work in groups, with each group making headbands for a particular character. Invite students to wear their headbands as you read the story again. Encourage them to pantomime the actions of their headband's character. You may want to have students wearing Cat, Dog, and Duck headbands say their character's lines aloud during the reading.

6 Read Other Versions

Gather other versions of *The Little Red Hen* to read to the students, and then lead them in comparing and contrasting the different versions.

7 Assign Roles and Practice Actions

For the role of Little Red Hen, you will need a student who is capable of remembering the order of events in the story. With their repeating lines, the roles of Cat, Dog, and Duck may be more appealing to students who have difficulty remembering and sequencing.

Have students look at their "Follow the Story" pictures as you review the story's main events with them. Invite students to suggest ways to act out these events. Then give them time to practice their actions.

8 Set Up Scenery and Props

Have as many props as possible for the steps in growing the wheat and making the bread. You may also want to give the dog a ball and give the duck a towel to help identify their characters and their activities in the story.

9 Retell the Story

Invite students to wear their headbands and retell the story in their own words. For each group of storytellers, introduce the story and its setting as a signal to begin.

10 Invite an Audience (optional)

When students are comfortable retelling the story, you may want to invite an audience to watch them and cheer them on. You will find a reproducible invitation on page 176.

Props
- Seeds
- Long pieces of straw or grass (for wheat)
- Flour
- Loaf of bread

After the Story
Reproduce page 53 for each student. Distribute the copies and help students complete the activities.

The Little Red Hen

One day on the farm, Little Red Hen was poking at the dirt with her beak. She found some wheat seeds. Little Red Hen called out, "Look! Some wheat! What a treat! Who will help me plant it?"

"Not I," said Cat. "I need to nap."
"Not I," said Dog. "I need to play."
"Not I," said Duck. "I need to swim."

So Little Red Hen planted the seeds all by herself.

After some time, the wheat grew. It was tall and yellow. Little Red Hen called out, "Look! Some wheat! What a treat! Who will help me cut it?"

"Not I," said Cat. "I need to nap."
"Not I," said Dog. "I need to play."
"Not I," said Duck. "I need to swim."

So Little Red Hen cut the wheat all by herself.

Because she knew that the best part of the wheat is the grain, Little Red Hen called out, "Look! Some wheat! What a treat! Who will help me thresh it?"

"Not I," said Cat. "I need to nap."
"Not I," said Dog. "I need to play."
"Not I," said Duck. "I need to swim."

So Little Red Hen threshed the wheat to get the grain all by herself.

She then called out, "Look! Grains of wheat! What a treat! Who will help me grind them?"

"Not I," said Cat. "I need to nap."
"Not I," said Dog. "I need to play."
"Not I," said Duck. "I need to swim."

So Little Red Hen ground the grain into flour all by herself.

She then called out, "Look! Flour from wheat! What a treat! Who will help me make some bread?"

"Not I," said Cat. "I need to nap."
"Not I," said Dog. "I need to play."
"Not I," said Duck. "I need to swim."

So Little Red Hen made the bread all by herself.

She then called out, "Look! Bread from wheat! What a treat! Who will help me eat it?"

"I will!" said Cat.
"I will!" said Dog.
"I will!" said Duck.

"Oh, no, you won't," said Little Red Hen. And she ate the bread all by herself!

Name _____

Meet the Characters

Trace the names.

hen

cat

dog

duck

Read and circle the answer.

I like to play.

I like to sleep.

Name _____

Follow the Story

Name _____

After the Story

Trace the sentence. Circle who said it.

Who will help me?

Listen and follow the directions.

1. Draw what Little Red Hen is eating.

2. Color the picture.

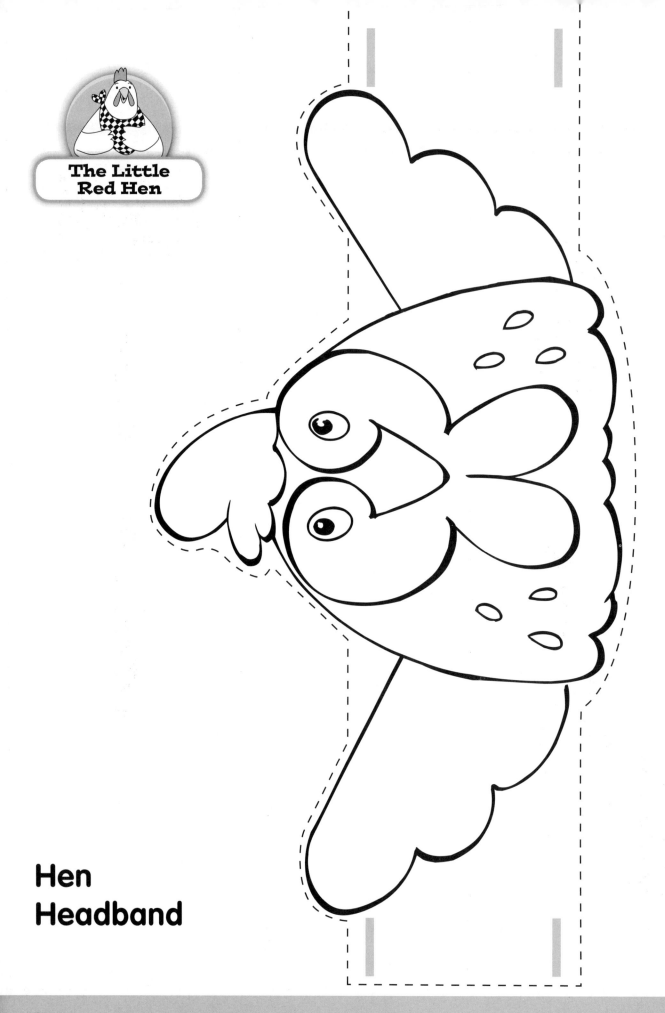

Hen
Headband

1. Cut out the three pieces of the headband. Cut along the dashed lines.

2. Staple the pieces together.

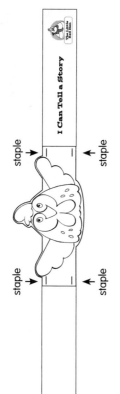

staple → ← staple

staple → ← staple

I Can Tell a Story

3. Fit the band around the student's head and staple the ends together.

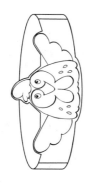

I Can Tell a Story

The Little
Red Hen

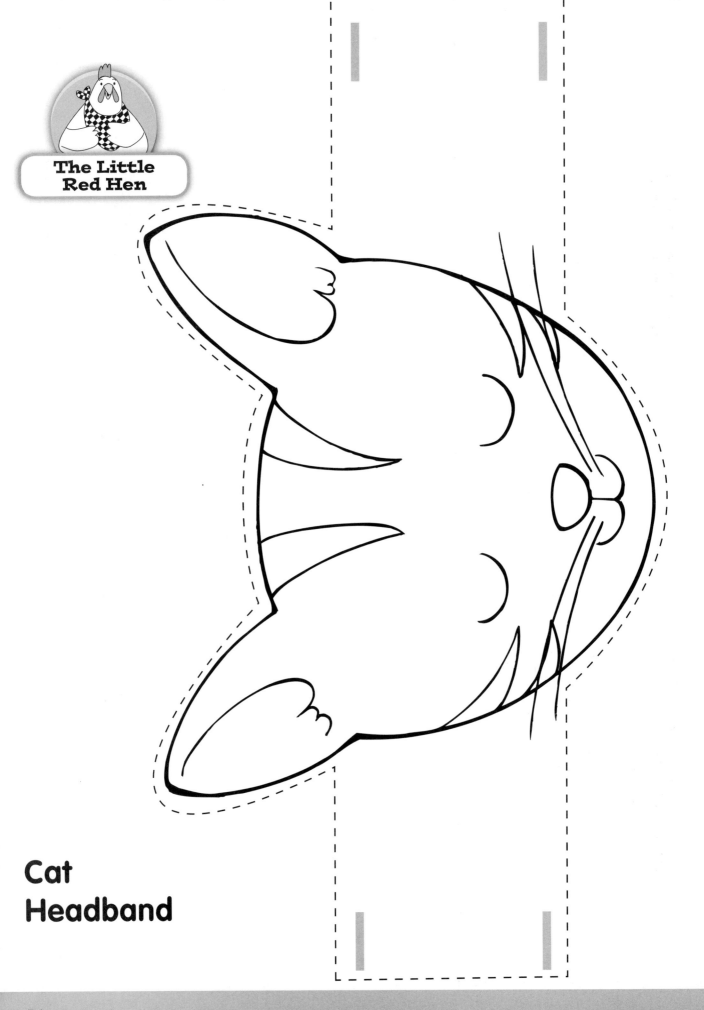

Cat
Headband

3 Fit the band around the student's head and staple the ends together.

1 Cut out the three pieces of the headband. Cut along the dashed lines.

2 Staple the pieces together.

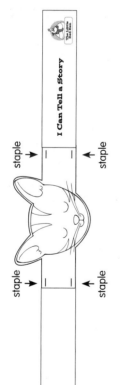

staple →

staple →

← staple

← staple

I Can Tell a Story

I Can Tell a Story

The Little Red Hen

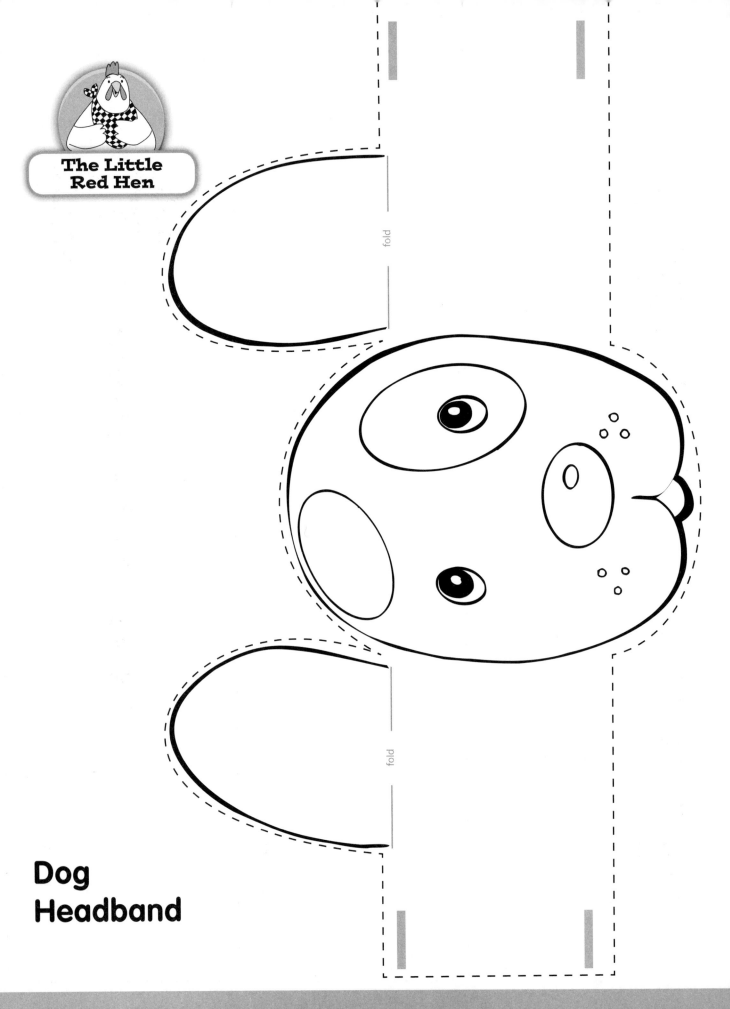

**The Little
Red Hen**

Dog
Headband

1 Cut out the three pieces of the headband.
Cut along the dashed lines.

2 Staple the pieces together.

3 Fold the ears forward.

4 Fit the band around the student's head and staple the ends together.

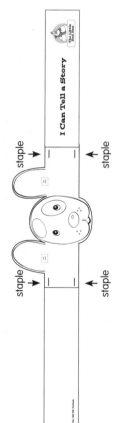

staple →

← staple

I Can Tell a Story

staple →

← staple

I Can Tell a Story

The Little Red Hen

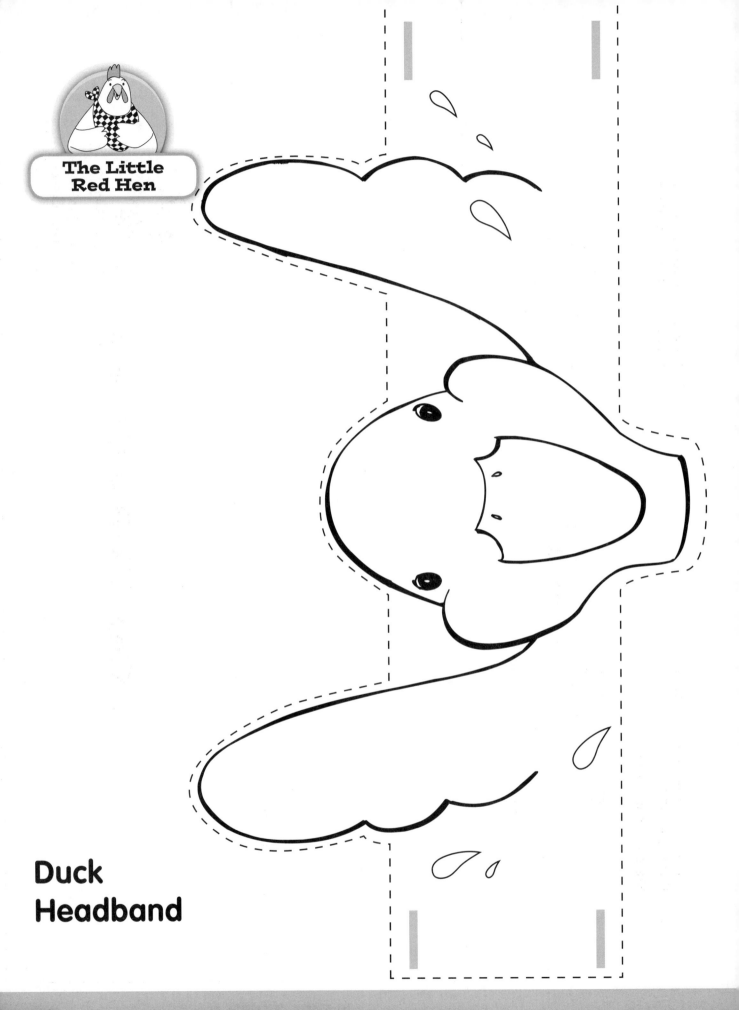

The Little
Red Hen

**Duck
Headband**

1 Cut out the three pieces of the headband.
Cut along the dashed lines.

2 Staple the pieces together.

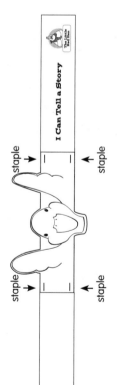

staple → ← staple

staple → ← staple

I Can Tell a Story

3 Fit the band around the student's
head and staple the ends together.

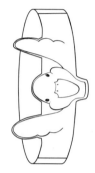

I Can Tell a Story

The Little
Red Hen

The Three Billy Goats Gruff

Three billy goats risk being eaten by a troll.

Handouts
Reproduce for each student.

- Meet the Characters
  Page 69

- Follow the Story
  Page 70

Headbands
Make a headband pattern for each student.

- Small Goat
  Pages 72 and 73

- Medium Goat
  Pages 74 and 75

- Big Goat
  Pages 76 and 77

- Troll
  Pages 78 and 79

1 Build Background

Distribute page 69 and tell students they will be hearing a make-believe story about three billy goats that meet up with a mean, ugly troll who wants to eat them. Have students point to each character on the page as you read its name. Share some relevant facts about the characters, such as that goats are animals that like to eat grass, and billy goats are boy goats. Trolls are make-believe people who are usually ugly, dirty, and mean and often live in caves or under bridges.

Guide students through the activities on the page. Then show them the first illustration in the story. Explain the goats' dilemma (crossing the bridge will get them to fresh grass but exposes them to a dangerous troll) and ask students to make predictions as to what the goats will do.

2 Read *The Three Billy Goats Gruff*

Read the story aloud. Show students the illustrations as you read. Change the pitch of your voice for each goat and use a gruff, mean tone for the troll. After reading the story, talk about the accuracy of the students' predictions.

3 Reread the Story

Distribute page 70. Tell students to look at the pictures on the page as you reread the story. The pictures are arranged and numbered in story sequence. When you come to an illustration in the story, have the students find the picture on the sheet that shows what you are reading about. Ask them to point to the picture. You may also want to ask them to tell you the number of the picture. Explain how the numbers can help them follow the story.

4 Talk About the Story

Have the students color the pictures on page 70. Encourage them to talk about what's happening in the pictures as they work.

5 Make Headbands

Give each student a headband pattern to color, cut out, and assemble. You may want to have the students work in groups, with each group making headbands for a particular character. Invite students to wear their headbands as you read the story again. Encourage them to pantomime the actions of their headband's character. You could also have the students tap their fingernails against a table or on the floor whenever a goat goes cloppity-clop over the bridge.

6 Read Other Versions

Gather other versions of *The Three Billy Goats Gruff* to read to the students, and then lead them in comparing and contrasting the different versions.

7 Assign Roles and Practice Actions

If possible, assign the roles of the goats to three students who are short, medium, and tall in size. You could choose either a boy or a girl to play the troll.

Have students look at their "Follow the Story" pictures as you review the story's main events with them. Invite students to suggest ways to act out these events. Then give them time to practice their actions.

8 Set Up Scenery and Props

A large table makes a sturdy bridge. If you're worried about safety, have the goats just pretend to walk over the bridge without actually climbing on the table. You may want to cover the table so the troll can hide under it and make a surprise entrance. Use the sign on page 68 to label the bridge. If you wish, you and the students could make grass out of large sheets of green construction paper. Place the grass to the right of the bridge to represent the hill of fresh grass.

9 Retell the Story

Invite students to wear their headbands and retell the story in their own words. For each group of storytellers, introduce the story and its setting as a signal to begin.

10 Invite an Audience (optional)

When students are comfortable retelling the story, you may want to invite an audience to watch them and cheer them on. You will find a reproducible invitation on page 176.

Props
- A large table
- "Bridge" sign (see page 68)
- Tall grass cut from large sheets of green construction paper (optional)

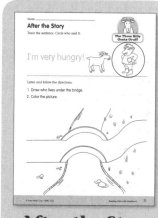

After the Story
Reproduce page 71 for each student. Distribute the copies and help students complete the activities.

The Three Billy Goats Gruff

Once upon a time, there were three gruff and grumpy billy goats. They were tired of eating the same old grass in the same old field. They could see a hill filled with fresh green grass. Oh, how the billy goats wanted to get to that hill! All they had to do was cross a bridge. Sounds simple, doesn't it?

But there was one problem—a big, mean, ugly problem. A big, mean, ugly troll lived under the bridge. And that troll loved to eat goats!

One day, the littlest goat said, "I cannot wait any longer. I have to go over the bridge. The grass on the hill looks so green and fresh!"

So the littlest billy goat went *cloppity, cloppity, clop* over the bridge. Just when he got to the middle, out jumped the mean, ugly troll.

"Who is making that racket?" the troll roared.

The little goat answered in a little goat voice. "It is I, the littlest goat. I want to get to the fresh green grass on the hill."

The troll yelled, "I'm hungry! I am going to eat you up!"

"Oh, no! Please don't eat me!" the goat squeaked. "I'm a thin little billy goat. You should wait for my brother. He is much bigger than I am, so he will be a tasty treat."

"Very well, Billy Goat, keep going before I change my mind!" shouted the troll. Then he slipped back under the bridge.

Retelling Tales with Headbands

Soon after, the middle-sized billy goat went *cloppity, cloppity, clop* over the bridge. Out jumped the mean, ugly troll.

"Who's making that racket?" he roared.

The middle-sized goat answered in a middle-sized voice. "It is I, the middle billy goat. I want to get to the fresh green grass on the hill."

"Well, I'm hungry! I am going to gobble you up!" yelled the troll.

"Oh, no! Please don't eat me," said the goat. "I am not very tender. I would be hard to chew. Wait for my big brother to come along. He's a plump and tender billy goat."

The troll began to drool at the thought of a big, juicy billy goat. "Very well," the troll shouted. "Keep going before I change my mind!" And the troll slipped back under the bridge.

Not long after, the biggest billy goat came *cloppity, cloppity, clop* over the bridge. Out jumped the mean, ugly troll.

"Who's making that racket?" he roared.

The big goat answered in a big goat voice. "It is I, the biggest billy goat. I want to get to the fresh green grass on the hill."

"I'm very hungry!" roared the troll. "I am going to eat you up!"

The biggest billy goat looked at the troll and smiled. Then the big goat lowered his head and rammed the troll with his big horns. The troll flew high into the air.

When the troll landed, he rolled over and over and over on the ground. And that big, mean, ugly troll is still rolling today!

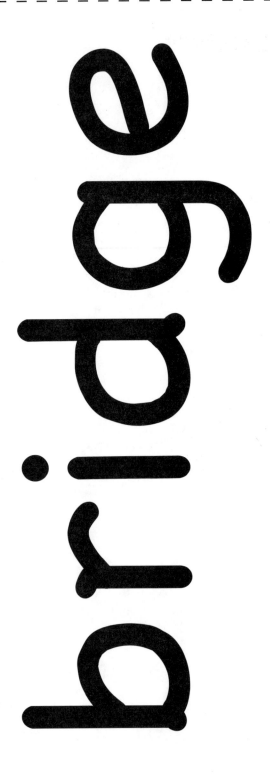

1 Reproduce and cut along dashed lines.

2 Tape sign to table.

Name _____

Meet the Characters

Trace the names.

goat 1

goat 2

goat 3

troll

Read and circle the answer.

I am real.

I am not real.

Name _____

Follow the Story

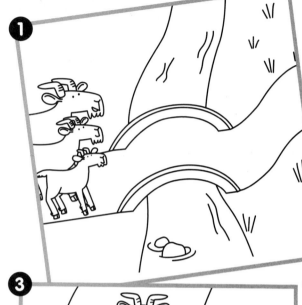

Name _____

After the Story

Trace the sentence. Circle who said it.

I'm very hungry!

Listen and follow the directions.

1. Draw who lives under the bridge.

2. Color the picture.

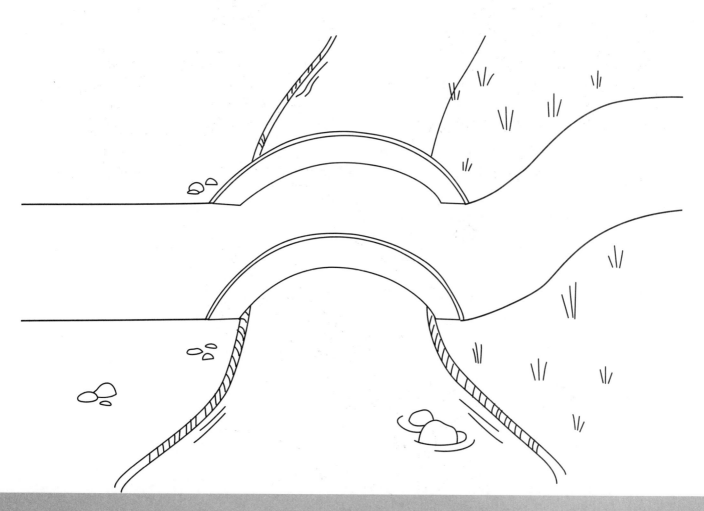

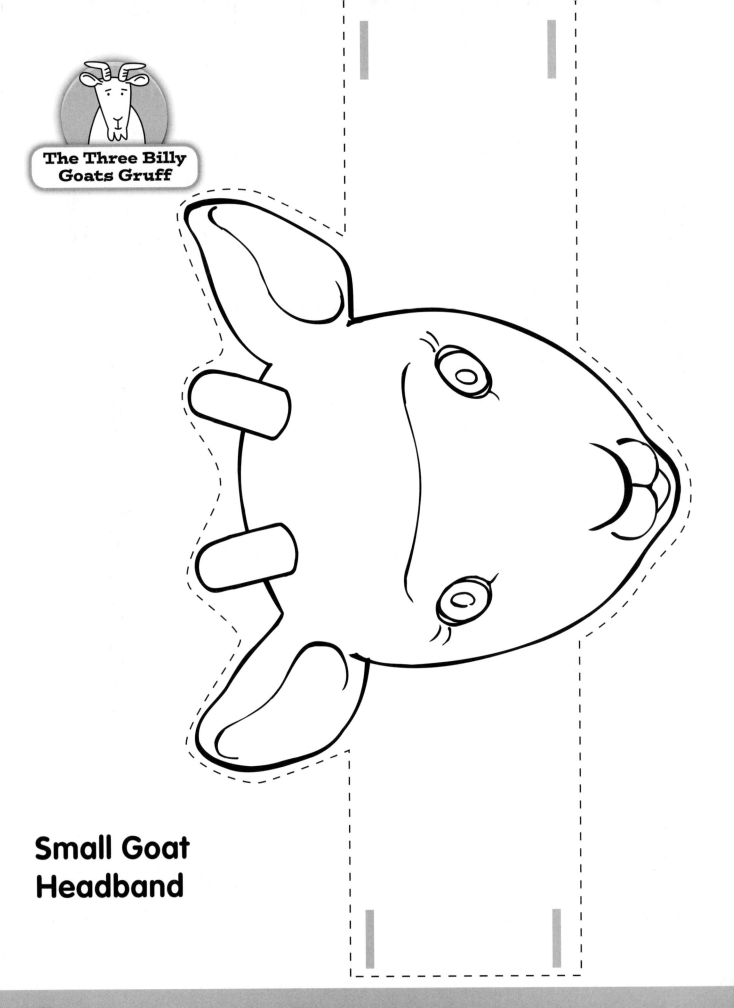

**The Three Billy
Goats Gruff**

Small Goat
Headband

1 Cut out the three pieces of the headband.
   Cut along the dashed lines.

2 Staple the pieces together.

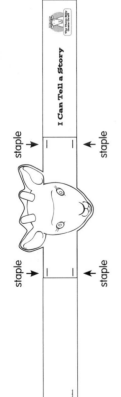

staple

staple

I Can Tell a Story

staple

staple

3 Fit the band around the student's head and staple the ends together.

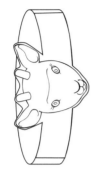

I Can Tell a Story

The Three Billy Goats Gruff

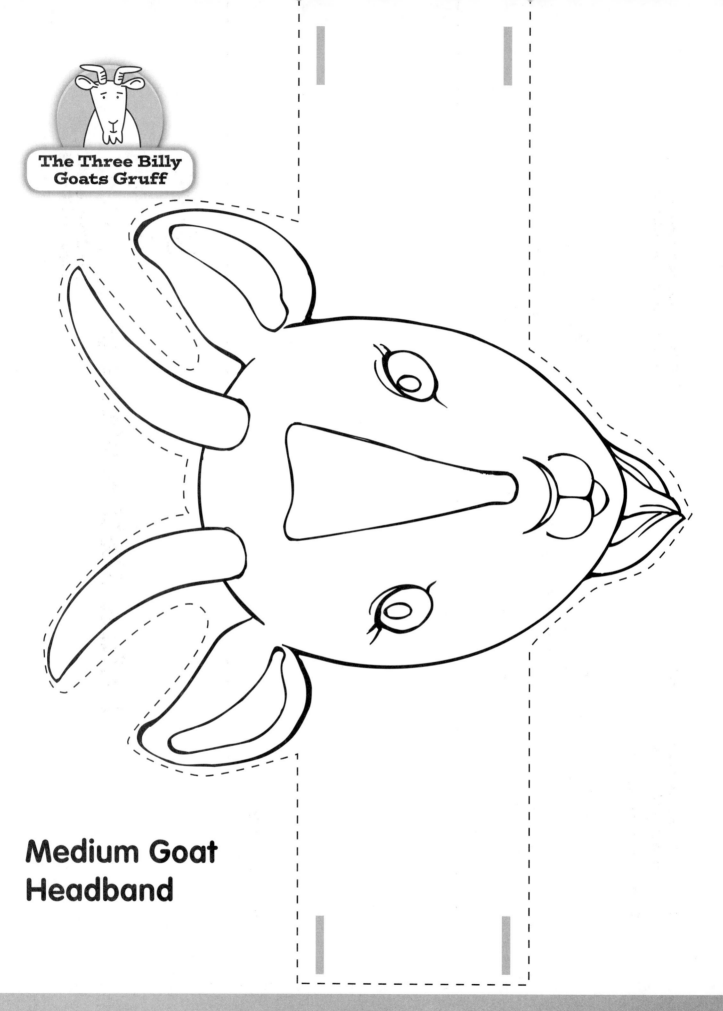

The Three Billy Goats Gruff

Medium Goat Headband

EMC 3322 • © Evan-Moor Corp.

1 Cut out the three pieces of the headband.
  Cut along the dashed lines.

2 Staple the pieces together.

3 Fit the band around the student's
  head and staple the ends together.

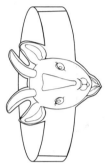

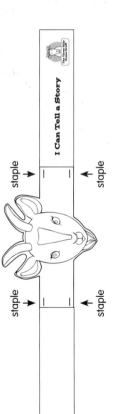

staple

staple

I Can Tell a Story

staple

staple

I Can Tell a Story

The Three Billy Goats Gruff

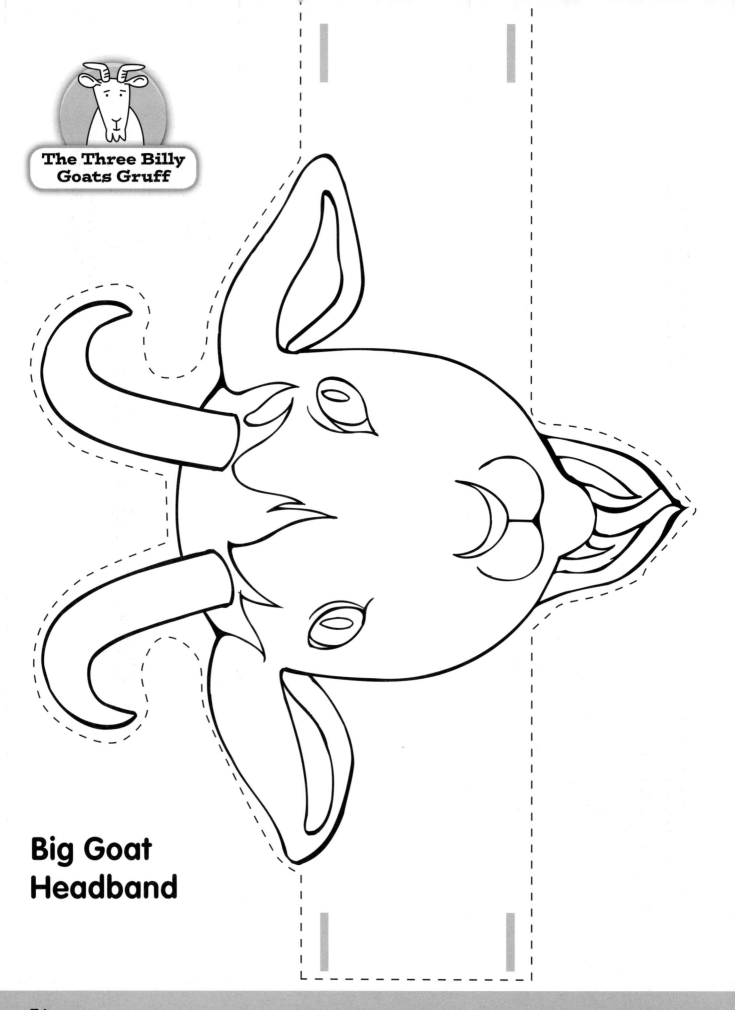

**The Three Billy
Goats Gruff**

Big Goat
Headband

3 Fit the band around the student's head and staple the ends together.

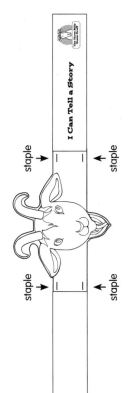

1 Cut out the three pieces of the headband. Cut along the dashed lines.

2 Staple the pieces together.

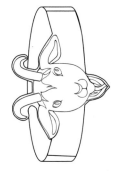

staple → ← staple

staple → ← staple

I Can Tell a Story

I Can Tell a Story

© Evan-Moor Corp. • EMC 3322

The Three Billy Goats Gruff

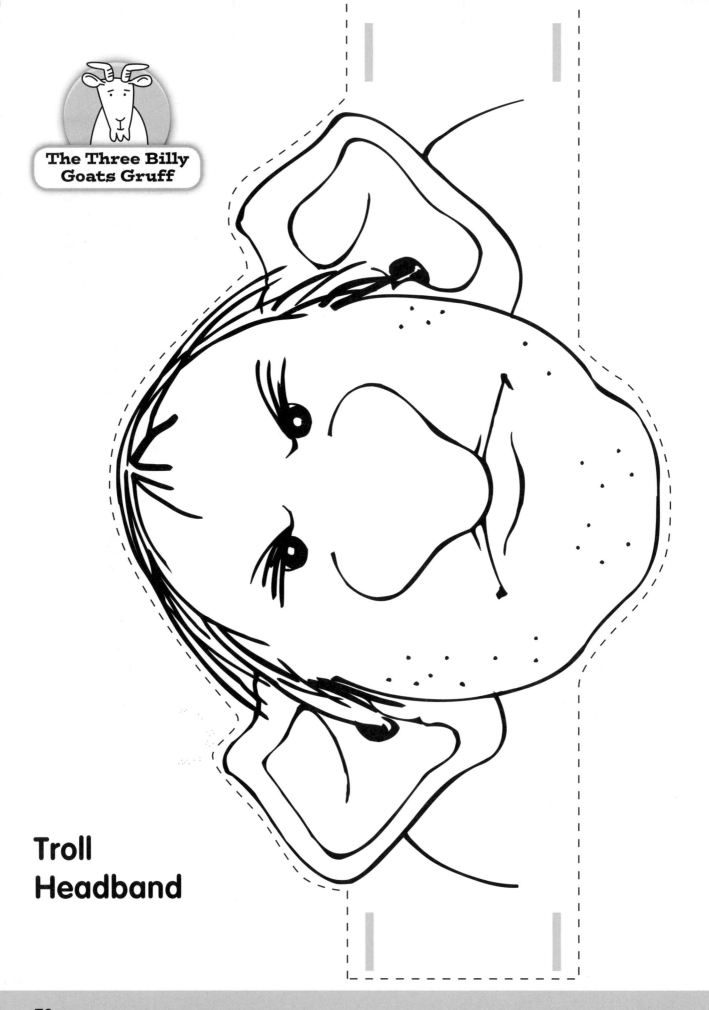

Troll Headband

3 Fit the band around the student's head and staple the ends together.

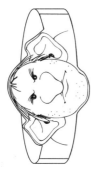

1 Cut out the three pieces of the headband. Cut along the dashed lines.

2 Staple the pieces together.

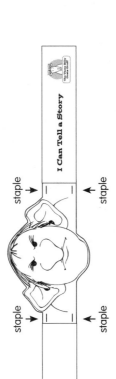

staple

staple

staple

staple

I Can Tell a Story

I Can Tell a Story

The Three Billy Goats Gruff

Retelling Tales with Headbands

Goldilocks and the Three Bears

A little girl snoops around inside a house in the woods and gets a big surprise.

Handouts

Reproduce for each student.

- Meet the Characters
  Page 87
- Follow the Story
  Page 88

Headbands

Make a headband pattern for each student.

- Papa Bear
  Pages 90 and 91
- Mama Bear
  Pages 92 and 93
- Baby Bear
  Pages 94 and 95
- Goldilocks
  Pages 96 and 97

1 Build Background

Distribute page 87 and tell students they will be hearing a make-believe story about a little girl whose curiosity gets her in trouble with a family of bears when she enters their house uninvited. Have students point to each character on the page as you read its name. Ask them to look closely at the pictures of the three bears and tell how the bears differ from each other.

Share some relevant facts about bears, such as that they live in dens (not houses), and they are meat-eaters, but they also eat lots of plants, including berries. Then guide students through the activities on the page.

2 Read *Goldilocks and the Three Bears*

Read the story aloud. Show students the illustrations as you read. Change the sound of your voice for each character. For example, use a deep voice for Papa Bear, a normal voice for Mama Bear, and a high-pitched voice for Baby Bear. Invite students to say "How about that!" with you each time it comes up in the story.

3 Reread the Story

Distribute page 88. Tell students to look at the pictures on the page as you reread the story. The pictures are arranged and numbered in story sequence. When you come to an illustration in the story, have the students find the picture on the sheet that shows what you are reading about. Ask them to point to the picture. You may also want to ask them to tell you the number of the picture. Explain how the numbers can help them follow the story.

4 Talk About the Story

Have the students color the pictures on page 88. Encourage them to talk about what's happening in the pictures as they work.

5 Make Headbands

Give each student a headband pattern to color, cut out, and assemble. You may want to have the students work in groups, with each group making headbands for a particular character. Invite students to wear their headbands as you read the story again. Encourage them to pantomime the actions of their headband's character.

6 Read Other Versions

Gather other versions of *The Three Bears* or *Goldilocks and the Three Bears* to read to the students, and then lead them in comparing and contrasting the different versions.

⑦ Assign Roles and Practice Actions

You may want to assign the role of Baby Bear to a boy or a girl who likes to act silly and doesn't mind playing a younger character. For the role of Goldilocks, choose a very expressive student who would be capable of exaggerating reactions.

Have students look at their "Follow the Story" pictures as you review the story's main events with them. Invite students to suggest ways to act out these events. Then give them time to practice their actions.

⑧ Set Up Scenery and Props

Designate a space for the inside of the bears' house. Place two chairs back to back with walking space between them for a doorway. Hang the "Our Home" sign *(see page 86)* on or near the doorway.

Because all the actions in the story can be pantomimed, props are not essential, but using the props suggested *(right)* may help students remember the sequence of events more easily as they retell the story. Use bowls, spoons, and chairs that are small, medium, and large in size. Place the bowls and spoons on a table, put the three chairs near the table, and lay the towels on the floor close by.

⑨ Retell the Story

Invite students to wear their headbands and retell the story in their own words. For each group of storytellers, introduce the story and its setting as a signal to begin.

⑩ Invite an Audience *(optional)*

When students are comfortable retelling the story, you may want to invite an audience to watch them and cheer them on. You will find a reproducible invitation on page 176.

Props
- 2 chairs *(for doorway)*
- "Our Home" sign *(see page 86)*
- 3 bowls
- 3 spoons
- 3 chairs
- 3 towels

After the Story
Reproduce page 89 for each student. Distribute the copies and help students complete the activities.

Goldilocks and the Three Bears

Once upon a time, there were three bears who lived in a house in the woods. In their house, everything that was big belonged to Papa Bear. Everything that was medium-sized belonged to Mama Bear. Everything that was little belonged to Baby Bear.

One morning, Papa Bear cooked some oatmeal. "Let's go for a walk in the woods while the oatmeal cools," said Papa Bear. "We can pick some berries. Berries will make our oatmeal taste sweet."

  EMC 3322 • © Evan-Moor Corp.

Once upon the same time, a curious little girl named Goldilocks went exploring all by herself. Deep in the woods, she saw a house. She peeked in the windows. No one was home, so she opened the door and walked right in. How about that!

Inside the house, Goldilocks saw three bowls of oatmeal on a table. Feeling very hungry, she grabbed a big spoon and began to eat the oatmeal in the big bowl.

"This oatmeal is too hot!" cried Goldilocks.

Next, she tried the oatmeal in the medium-sized bowl. "This oatmeal is too cold!" she complained.

Then, she tasted the oatmeal in the little bowl. "This oatmeal is just right," she said.

Goldilocks ate every bit of the oatmeal in the little bowl. How about that!

Feeling very full, Goldilocks decided to sit and rest for a while. She saw three chairs. First, she sat down in the big chair.

"This chair is too hard," she said.

So Goldilocks sat down in the medium-sized chair. "This chair is too soft," she complained.

Finally, she sat down in the little chair. "This chair is just right," said Goldilocks, and she bounced up and down with delight. She bounced up and down so much that the little chair broke all to pieces. How about that!

Feeling sleepy, Goldilocks went into the bedroom. First, she laid down on the big bed. "The pillow on this bed is too flat," said Goldilocks.

Next, she tried the medium-sized bed. "The pillow on this bed is too fluffy," she complained. Finally, she tried the little bed. "This bed is just right," said Goldilocks. She covered herself with the blanket and fell fast asleep. How about that!

Goldilocks did not know that the house belonged to three bears. And she did not hear the bears come home.

Papa Bear was the first to see that something was not right. He saw his big spoon sticking up in his big bowl of oatmeal. "Somebody has been eating my oatmeal!" roared Papa Bear. Then, Mama Bear saw her medium-sized spoon in her medium-sized bowl. "Somebody has been eating my oatmeal!" she growled. Baby Bear turned over his little bowl and cried, "Somebody ate ALL of my oatmeal!"

Then the bears saw their chairs. "Somebody has been sitting in my chair!" roared Papa Bear. "Somebody has been sitting in my chair!" growled Mama Bear. "Somebody sat in my chair," cried Baby Bear, "and now it's broken!"

EMC 3322 • © Evan-Moor Corp.

The bears cautiously peeked into the bedroom. "Somebody has been sleeping in my bed!" Papa Bear roared.

"Somebody has been sleeping in my bed, too!" Mama Bear growled.

"Somebody IS sleeping in my bed!" cried Baby Bear. "Look! Here she is!"

The sound of the bears' voices was as loud as thunder. Goldilocks woke up with her heart pounding. When she saw the three angry bears, she screamed.

Goldilocks tumbled out of bed, ran down the stairs, and dashed out the door. And she never, ever went exploring by herself in the woods again. How about that!

Retelling Tales with Headbands

Our Home

1 Reproduce and cut along dashed line.

2 Hang on or near doorway of bears' home.

Name _____

Meet the Characters

Trace the names.

papa

mama

baby

Goldilocks

Read and circle the answer.

I am a girl.

We live together.

Name _____

Follow the Story

Goldilocks and the Three Bears

1

2

3

4

5

EMC 3322 • © Evan-Moor Corp.

Name _____

After the Story

Trace the sentence. Circle who said it.

Goldilocks and the Three Bears

Here she is!

Listen and follow the directions.

1. Draw where the three bears found Goldilocks.

2. Color the picture.

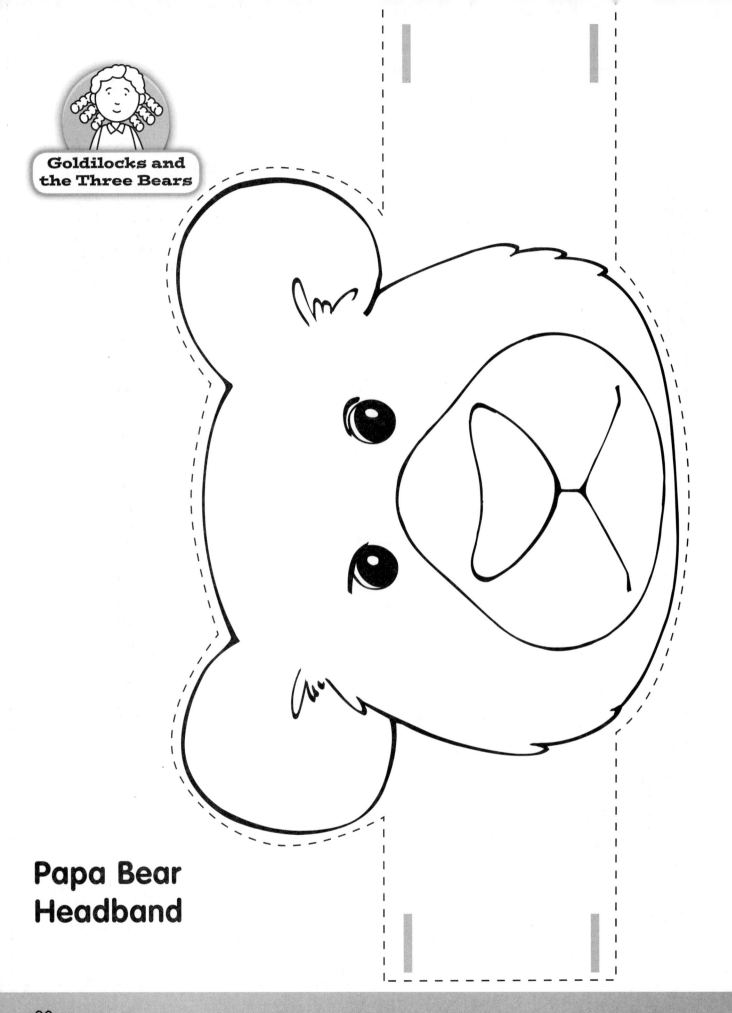

Goldilocks and the Three Bears

Papa Bear
Headband

1 Cut out the three pieces of the headband.
Cut along the dashed lines.

2 Staple the pieces together.

3 Fit the band around the student's head and staple the ends together.

staple →   ← staple

I Can Tell a Story

staple →   ← staple

I Can Tell a Story

Goldilocks and the Three Bears

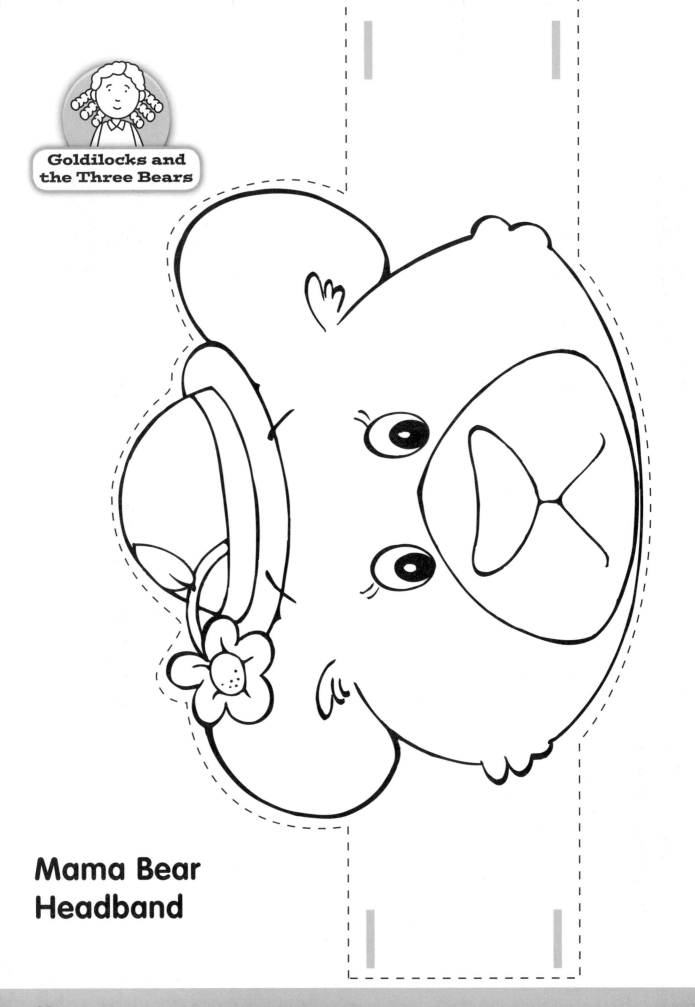

Mama Bear Headband

① Cut out the three pieces of the headband.
   Cut along the dashed lines.

② Staple the pieces together.

③ Fit the band around the student's head and staple the ends together.

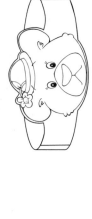

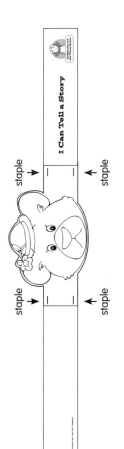

staple →

← staple

I Can Tell a Story

staple →

← staple

I Can Tell a Story

Goldilocks and the Three Bears

Goldilocks and the Three Bears

Baby Bear
Headband

Retelling Tales with Headbands

1. Cut out the three pieces of the headband.
   Cut along the dashed lines.
2. Staple the pieces together.

3. Fit the band around the student's
   head and staple the ends together.

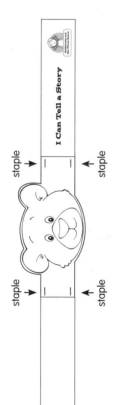

staple →

staple →

← staple

← staple

I Can Tell a Story

I Can Tell a Story

**Goldilocks and
the Three Bears**

Goldilocks and the Three Bears

Goldilocks Headband

1 Cut out the three pieces of the headband.
   Cut along the dashed lines.

2 Staple the pieces together.

3 Fit the band around the student's
   head and staple the ends together.

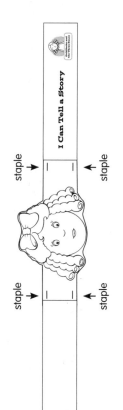

staple → ← staple

staple → ← staple

I Can Tell a Story

I Can Tell a Story

Goldilocks and
the Three Bears

The Three Little Pigs

*Three pigs each build a house, but only
one of them thinks about safety.*

Handouts

*Reproduce for each
student.*

- Meet the
  Characters
  Page 105

- Follow the Story
  Page 106

Headbands

*Make a headband
pattern for each
student.*

- First Pig
  Pages 108 and 109

- Second Pig
  Pages 110 and 111

- Third Pig
  Pages 112 and 113

- Wolf
  Pages 114 and 115

1 Build Background

Distribute page 105 and tell students they will be hearing a make-believe
story about three pigs that build houses and a big bad wolf that comes to
their houses. Have students look carefully at the illustrations of the three
pigs. Ask them to compare the pictures and tell you how they are different.

Share some relevant facts about the characters, such as that pigs are smart
animals, and they can run almost as fast as squirrels, and that a wolf is a
wild animal that can see, hear, and smell very well and eats other animals.
Then guide students through the activities on the page.

2 Read *The Three Little Pigs*

Read the story aloud. Show students the illustrations as you read. Use a
different pitch or tone of voice for each character, especially the wolf. Invite
students to huff and puff along with the wolf when you read those lines.
You may also want to divide the students into two choruses, with one chorus
saying the wolf's rhyming lines and the other saying the pigs' responses.

3 Reread the Story

Distribute page 106. Tell students to look at the pictures on the page as you
reread the story. The pictures are arranged and numbered in story sequence.
When you come to an illustration in the story, have the students find the
picture on the sheet that shows what you are reading about. Ask them to
point to the picture. You may also want to ask them to tell you the number
of the picture. Explain how the numbers can help them follow the story.

4 Talk About the Story

Have the students color the pictures on page 106. Encourage them to talk
about what's happening in the pictures as they work.

5 Make Headbands

Give each student a headband pattern to color, cut out, and assemble. You
may want to have the students work in groups, with each group making
headbands for a particular character. You could also have students make
the signs on page 104. The signs are for the characters who give the straw,
sticks, and bricks to the pigs at the beginning of the story. The signs can be
worn, carried, or used instead of actual props *(see page 99)*. Invite students
to wear their headbands or signs as you read the story again. Encourage
them to pantomime the actions of their headband's or sign's character.

6 Read Other Versions

Gather other versions of *The Three Little Pigs* to read to the students, such
as *The Three Little Pigs* by James Marshall and *The Three Little Wolves and the
Big Bad Pig* by Eugene Trivizas. Lead students in comparing and contrasting
the different versions.

7 Assign Roles and Practice Actions

All of the roles in this story are suitable for either boys or girls.
For example, the three pigs could be sisters instead of brothers.
Encourage even typically shy students to be the wolf. The actions
and rhyming lines for that role are easy to learn and remember.

Have students look at their "Follow the Story" pictures as you review
the story's main events with them. Invite students to suggest ways
to act out these events. Then give them time to practice their actions.

8 Set Up Scenery and Props

Making the pigs' houses can be as simple as drawing three house
shapes on the board. After getting their straw, sticks, or bricks, the
pigs could simply stand in front of the drawings. Another way to
represent a pig's house is to have two or three students hold hands
and form a circle around the pig. When the wolf blows the house
to bits, the students simply unclasp their hands to break the circle
and move out of the scene, while the pig runs to the next house.

9 Retell the Story

Invite students to wear their headbands and retell the story in their
own words. For each group of storytellers, introduce the story and
its setting as a signal to begin.

10 Invite an Audience *(optional)*

When students are comfortable retelling the story, you may want to
invite an audience to watch them and cheer them on. You will find
a reproducible invitation on page 176.

Props
- "Straw," "Sticks," "Bricks" signs *(see page 104)*
- Clump of straw
- Handful of sticks
- Small boxes painted to look like bricks

After the Story
Reproduce page 107 for each student. Distribute the copies and help students complete the activities.

The Three Little Pigs

This is the story of three little pigs who thought they were all grown up. They waved good-bye to their family and went off on their own. Each pig wanted to build a fine house.

The first little pig met a man carrying a load of straw. The pig asked, "Please, sir, may I have that straw to build a house?"

"Yes, little pig. Yes, you may. This straw makes me itch anyway," said the man. The first pig took the straw and quickly built a straw house.

The second little pig met a man carrying a bundle of sticks. The pig asked, "Please, sir, may I have those sticks to build a house?"

"Yes, little pig. Yes, you may. These sticks poke me anyway," said the man. In no time at all, the second pig built a house of sticks. His house was right next door to his brother's house of straw.

The third little pig met a man who had some bricks. "Please, sir," asked the pig, "may I have those bricks to build a house?"

"Yes, little pig. Yes, you may. These bricks are heavy anyway," said the man. The third pig slowly and carefully built a brick house next door to his brothers' houses.

One day, the first pig was just sitting down to eat some corn mush pie when, all of a sudden, there was a loud knock on the door.

"Little pig, little pig, let me in!" called a big bad wolf.

"Not by the hair of my chinny, chin, chin," answered the frightened little pig. His voice was very shaky.

"Then, I'll huff, and I'll puff, and I'll blow your house in!" said the wolf.

The big bad wolf huffed, and he puffed, and, of course, he blew the straw house to bits!

Straw flew everywhere! But there was no little pig. You see, as the straw flew this way and that, the little pig ran to his brother's house of sticks.

The big bad wolf was very angry! He tromped over to the house of sticks and knocked on the door. "Little pig, little pig, let me in!" he yelled.

"Not by the hair on my chinny, chin, chin!" squealed the second pig.

"Then I'll huff, and I'll puff, and I'll blow your house in!" growled the wolf. The big bad wolf huffed, and he puffed, and, of course, he blew the stick house to bits!

Sticks flew everywhere! But there were no little pigs. You see, as the sticks flew this way and that, the two little pigs ran to their brother's house of bricks.

Now the big bad wolf was furious! He stomped over to the brick house and banged on the door.

"Little pig, little pig, let me in!" he howled.

"Not by the hair on my chinny, chin, chin," said the third pig. He turned to his brothers and winked.

"Then," screamed the wolf, "I'll huff, and I'll puff, and I'll blow your house in!"

EMC 3322 • © Evan-Moor Corp.

The big bad wolf huffed and he puffed, and he huffed and he puffed, and, of course, he could *not* blow the house of bricks to bits. The bricks did not move even one little bit.

Finally, the wolf gave up, and he crawled away, never to be seen again.

The three little pigs all cheered. "Hooray! The brick house is where we all will stay!"

straw

sticks

bricks

1. Reproduce and cut along dashed lines.

2. Glue each sign onto a 4-by-8-inch (10-by-20-cm) piece of colored construction paper.

straw

Name _____

Meet the Characters

Trace the names.

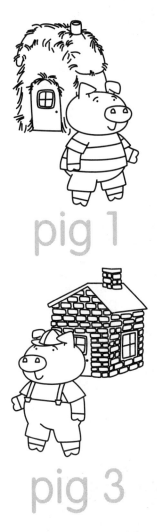

pig 1

pig 2

pig 3

wolf

Read and circle the answer.

There are 3 of us.

I huff and puff.

Name _____

Follow the Story

Name _____

After the Story

Trace the sentence. Circle who said it.

Let me in!

Listen and follow the directions.

1. Draw the house the three pigs live in at the end of the story.

2. Color the picture.

The Three Little Pigs

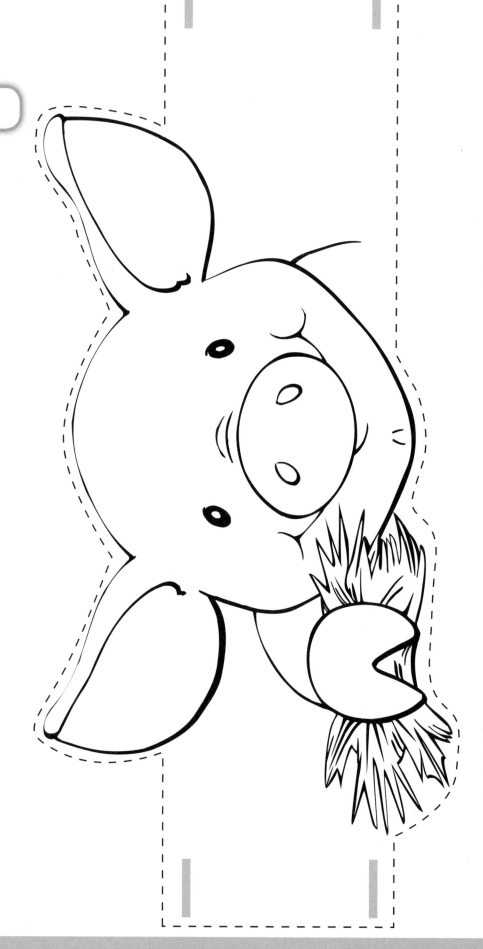

First Pig
Headband

1 Cut out the three pieces of the headband.
   Cut along the dashed lines.

2 Staple the pieces together.

3 Fit the band around the student's head and staple the ends together.

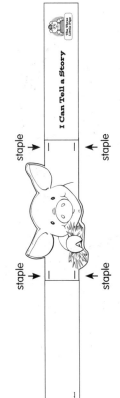

I Can Tell a Story

The Three Little Pigs

I Can Tell a Story

The Three Little Pigs

The Three Little Pigs

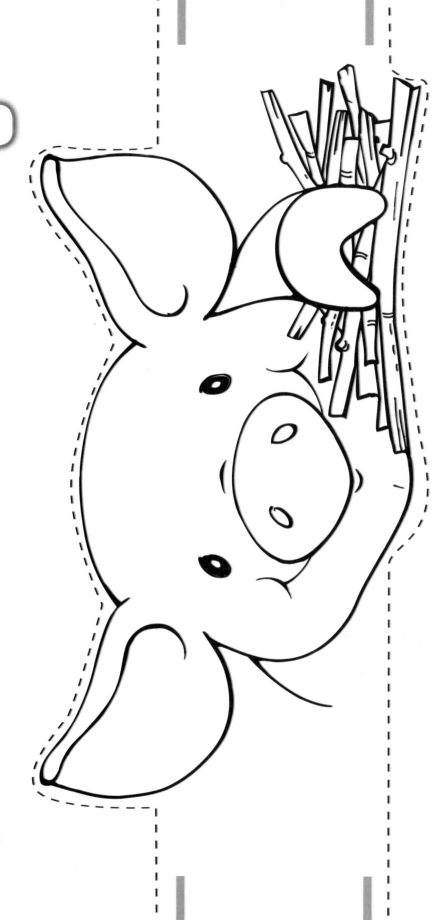

Second Pig Headband

1. Cut out the three pieces of the headband.
Cut along the dashed lines.
2. Staple the pieces together.
3. Fit the band around the student's head and staple the ends together.

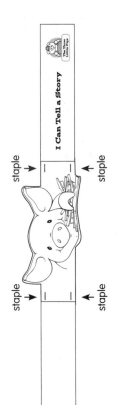

staple
staple
staple
staple

I Can Tell a Story

I Can Tell a Story

The Three
Little Pigs

The Three Little Pigs

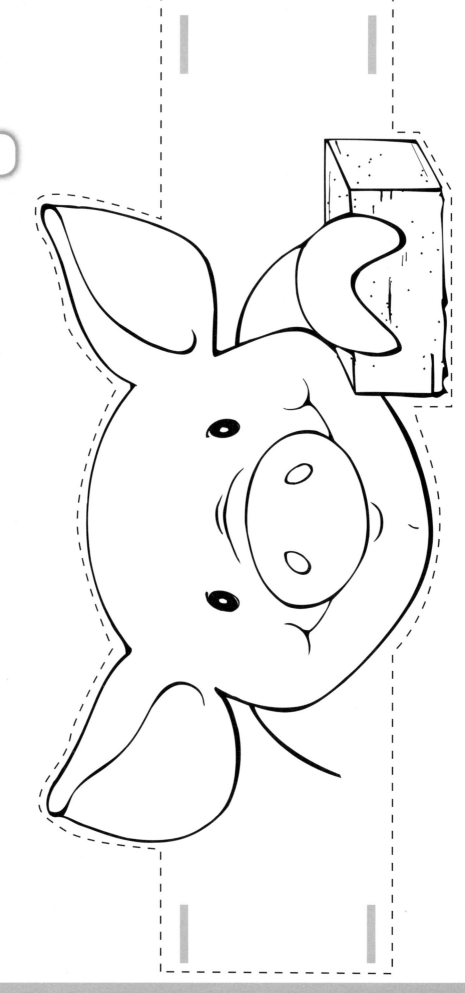

Third Pig Headband

1 Cut out the three pieces of the headband.
Cut along the dashed lines.

2 Staple the pieces together.

3 Fit the band around the student's head and staple the ends together.

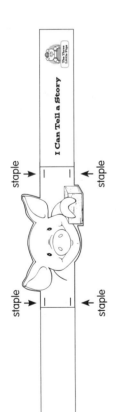

staple → ← staple

staple → ← staple

I Can Tell a Story

I Can Tell a Story

The Three Little Pigs

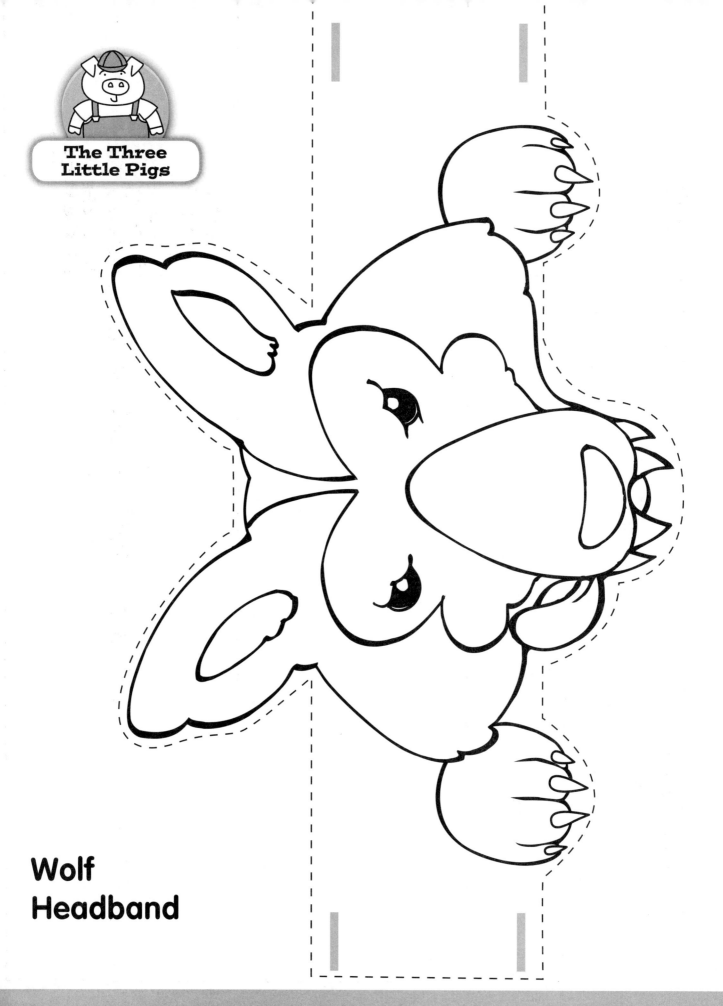

The Three Little Pigs

Wolf Headband

1. Cut out the three pieces of the headband.
   Cut along the dashed lines.

2. Staple the pieces together.

3. Fit the band around the student's head and staple the ends together.

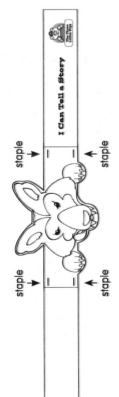

staple →

← staple

staple →

← staple

I Can Tell a Story

I Can Tell a Story

The Three Little Pigs

Jack and the Beanstalk

Jack sells the family cow for five magic beans that take him to an adventure high in the sky.

Handouts

Reproduce for each student.

- Meet the Characters
  Page 123

- Follow the Story
  Page 124

Headbands

Make a headband pattern for each student.

- Jack
  Pages 126 and 127

- Jack's Mother
  Pages 128 and 129

- Giant's Wife
  Pages 130 and 131

- Giant
  Pages 132 and 133

1 Build Background

Distribute page 123 and tell students they will be hearing a make-believe story about a boy named Jack. Have students point to Jack's picture as you tell them a simple fact about Jack that helps reveal the storyline, such as that Jack trades a cow for some magic beans. Do the same for each of the other characters. Then guide students through the activities on the page.

Next, explain that the beanstalk grew from Jack's beans after his mother threw them onto the ground. Talk about how beans grow, and then have the students pretend to be small beans growing into tall beanstalks. First, ask them to squat and curl their bodies into small shapes. Then have them stand slowly and stretch upward as high as they can.

2 Read *Jack and the Beanstalk*

Read the story aloud. Show students the illustrations as you read. To play up the giant's scariness, use a loud, gruff voice for the giant and a much softer voice for Jack. Invite students to echo or join in on the "Fee-fi-fo-fum" rhyme.

3 Reread the Story

Distribute page 124. Tell students to look at the pictures on the page as you reread the story. The pictures are arranged and numbered in story sequence. When you come to an illustration in the story, have the students find the picture on the sheet that shows what you are reading about. Ask them to point to the picture. You may also want to ask them to tell you the number of the picture. Explain how the numbers can help them follow the story.

4 Talk About the Story

Have the students color the pictures on page 124. Encourage them to talk about what's happening in the pictures as they work.

5 Make Headbands

Give each student a headband pattern to color, cut out, and assemble. You may want to have the students work in groups, with each group making headbands for a particular character. Invite students to wear their headbands as you read the story again. Encourage them to pantomime the actions of their headband's character. You could also have them drum with the palms of their hands on the classroom tables or on the floor to make the giant's thumping sounds.

6 Read Other Versions

Gather other versions of *Jack and the Beanstalk* to read to the students, and then lead them in comparing and contrasting the different versions.

(7) Assign Roles and Practice Actions

Assign the role of Jack to a student who has the ability to remember a lot of dialogue and perform a variety of expressions. For the giant, you may want to choose someone who does not already tend to be excluded by others. Keep in mind that the man with the beans could be a woman instead.

Have students look at their "Follow the Story" pictures as you review the story's main events with them. Invite students to suggest ways to act out these events. Then give them time to practice their actions.

(8) Set Up Scenery and Props

Use a large table for the giant's castle. The rest of the action can take place to one side of the table. Students can just pantomime climbing a beanstalk, or they can color or paint one on a long piece of butcher paper. Either tape up the paper beanstalk between Jack and the giant's castle or have students hold it. Color and cut out the golden hen template on page 122. Attach the hen to a large craft stick to make it easy to carry. Be sure that the student playing the man who buys Jack's cow has five beans in his or her pocket.

(9) Retell the Story

Invite students to wear their headbands and retell the story in their own words. For each group of storytellers, introduce the story and its setting as a signal to begin.

(10) Invite an Audience *(optional)*

When students are comfortable retelling the story, you may want to invite an audience to watch them and cheer them on. You will find a reproducible invitation on page 176.

Props
- Large table
- Golden hen *(see page 122)*
- 5 large beans (use dried beans or jelly beans)

After the Story
Reproduce page 125 for each student. Distribute the copies and help students complete the activities.

Jack and the Beanstalk

Once upon a magical time, a boy named Jack lived with his mother in a little house. They were very poor, and one sad day, they had to sell their cow to get money for food.

"Take the cow into town and get as much money for it as you can," Jack's mother told him.

Jack and the cow started walking to town. They had not gone far when they met a man. "Where are you going?" asked the man.

Jack said, "I'm going to town to sell my cow."

The man reached deep into his pocket and pulled out five large beans. "I will trade you these beans for your cow," he said. "These are not ordinary beans. These beans are magic."

Jack's eyes opened wide. "Magic beans!" he cried. "Yes, you can have my cow!" Jack snatched the beans out of the man's hands and ran home.

Retelling Tales with Headbands   EMC 3322 • © Evan-Moor Corp.

"Mother! Mother!" Jack shouted. "Look what I got for the cow!" He proudly showed her the magic beans.

Jack's mother did not smile. "What?" she yelled. "You sold the cow for five beans! How can we live on that?" Jack's mother grabbed the beans and threw them out the window. She sent Jack straight to bed. Then she sat down and cried.

When Jack woke up the next morning, his room was still dark. Huge leaves blocked the sun from shining through the window. Jack quickly dressed and went outside. The beans his mother had thrown out the window had grown, overnight, into a beanstalk that reached far into the sky!

"The beans were magic!" thought Jack.

Right away, Jack began to climb the beanstalk. Up and up he went, higher than the treetops, higher than the hills, higher than the birds. Jack climbed high into the clouds. At last, he reached the top. And what do you think he saw?

Jack saw a huge castle. He boldly walked up to the castle and knocked on the door. A tall woman opened it.

"Hello," said Jack. "I'm very hungry and very tired. Could you please give me something to eat and a place to rest?"

"Get out of here!" hissed the woman. "This is no place for a boy. My husband is a giant. He would eat you in one bite!"

"But I've come such a long way," Jack begged.

The woman had a kind heart. Quickly and quietly, she took Jack into the biggest kitchen he had ever seen. She gave him bread and cheese and apples to eat. Jack was taking his last mouthful when... THUMP! THUMP! **THUMP!**

The noise came closer and closer to the kitchen.
THUMP! THUMP! THUMP!

The woman pushed Jack onto a cupboard and closed the door. She was just in time, too, because the giant thumped into the kitchen the very next minute. He stopped at the cupboard where Jack was hiding. Then he sniffed the air and shouted,

Fee-fi-fo-fum!
I smell a little boy!
Yum! Yum! Yum!

"There is no boy in here," the woman told the giant. "You just smell the sausages I'm cooking."

Jack peeked through a crack in the cupboard door. He watched the giant eat 100 sausages and 50 eggs.

Then the giant yelled, "Wife, fetch me my golden hen!"

The woman left the room and came back with a hen that had feathers made of gold. She placed the hen on the table. The giant stroked the hen's back and roared "Lay!" To Jack's surprise, the golden hen laid a golden egg!

EMC 3322 • © Evan-Moor Corp.

After playing with the hen, the giant fell deep asleep. Jack tiptoed over to the table. "I wish I had a hen like that for my mother," he whispered.

"Take the hen," said the woman. "But hurry! Get out of here before the giant wakes up."

Jack climbed onto the table and grabbed the golden hen. Then he jumped down and ran as fast as his legs could carry him. Just as Jack got to the castle door, the hen squawked and woke the giant.

"Where is my hen?" the giant roared.

Holding the golden hen tightly, Jack rushed out the door, ran to the beanstalk, and climbed down. The giant followed Jack with giant steps, but he was so heavy that he moved very slowly down the beanstalk. BUMP. BUMP. BUMP.

"Mother! Mother!" shouted Jack when he got to the bottom of the beanstalk. "Get an ax. Hurry!"

Jack's mother ran out of the house, carrying an ax. CHOP! CHOP! CHOP! The beanstalk fell with a crash, and so did the giant.

Jack and his mother were safe. And, because they had the golden hen, they were never poor again.

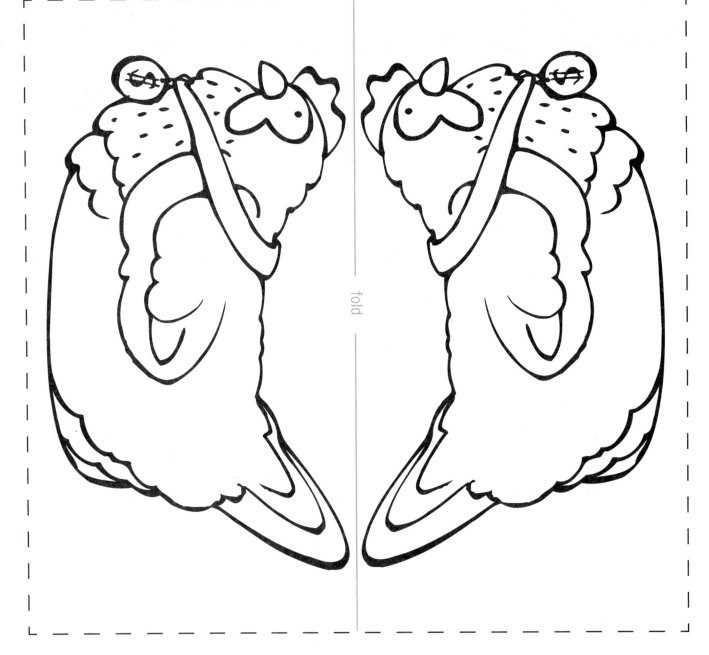

fold

1. Reproduce and cut along dashed lines.

2. Fold in half along center line.

3. Glue the top part of a large craft stick between the folded sheets.

Name _____

Meet the Characters

Trace the names.

Jack and the
Beanstalk

Jack

mother

giant's wife

giant

Read and circle the answer.

I am a boy.

I am very big.

Name _____

Follow the Story

Jack and the Beanstalk

Name _____

After the Story

Trace the sentence. Circle who said it.

Jack and the Beanstalk

Where is my hen?

Listen and follow the directions.

1. Draw what Jack climbed.

2. Color the picture.

Jack and the Beanstalk

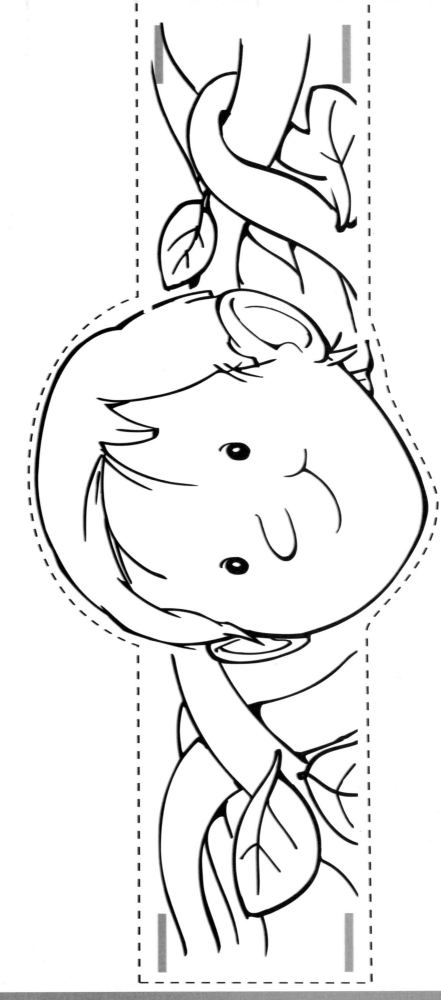

Jack
Headband

1 Cut out the three pieces of the headband.
   Cut along the dashed lines.

2 Staple the pieces together.

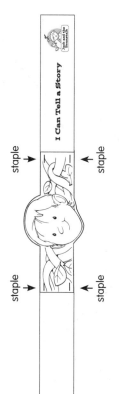

3 Fit the band around the student's
   head and staple the ends together.

I Can Tell a Story

Jack and the
Beanstalk

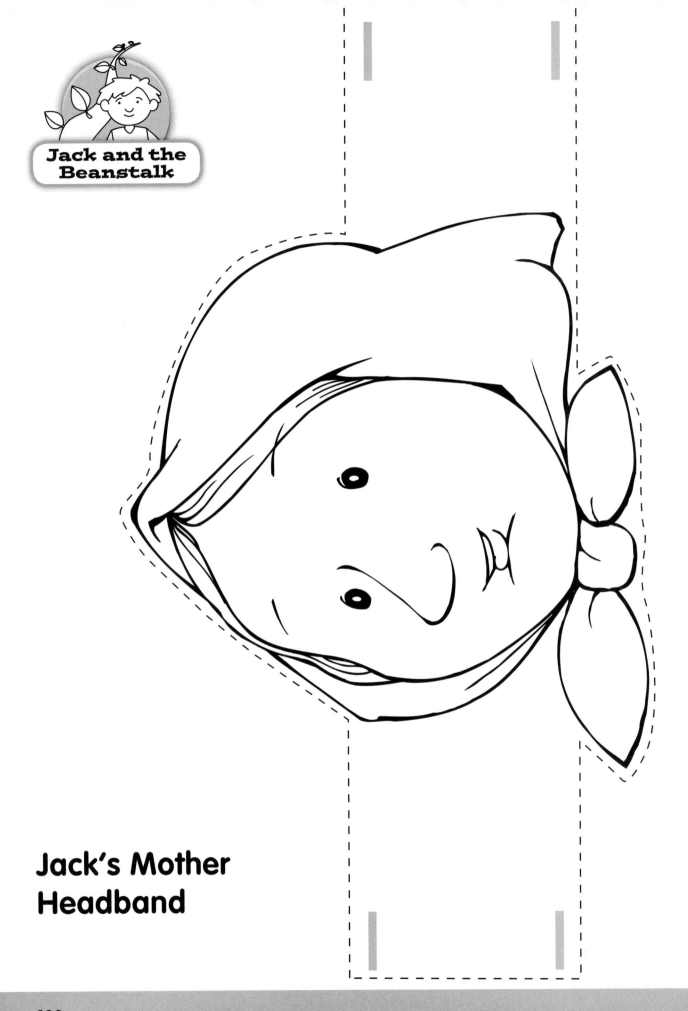

**Jack's Mother
Headband**

Retelling Tales with Headbands

1 Cut out the three pieces of the headband.
   Cut along the dashed lines.

2 Staple the pieces together.

3 Fit the band around the student's
   head and staple the ends together.

staple →

← staple

I Can Tell a Story

staple →

← staple

I Can Tell a Story

Jack and the
Beanstalk

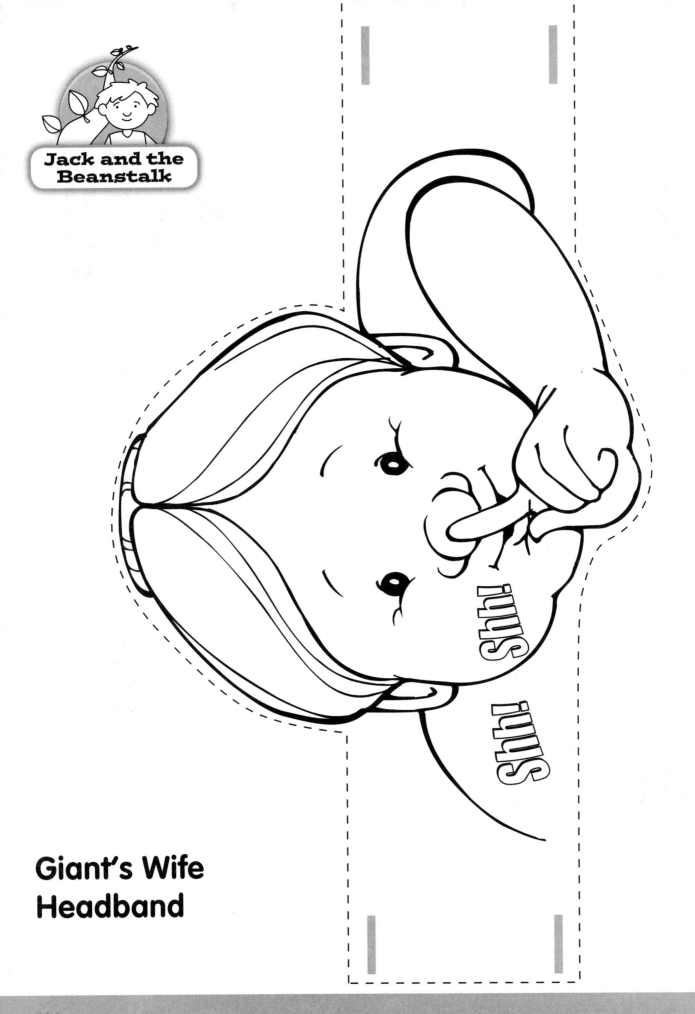

Giant's Wife Headband

1 Cut out the three pieces of the headband.
  Cut along the dashed lines.

2 Staple the pieces together.

3 Fit the band around the student's head and staple the ends together.

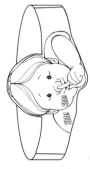

staple → ← staple

I Can Tell a Story

staple → ← staple

I Can Tell a Story

Jack and the Beanstalk

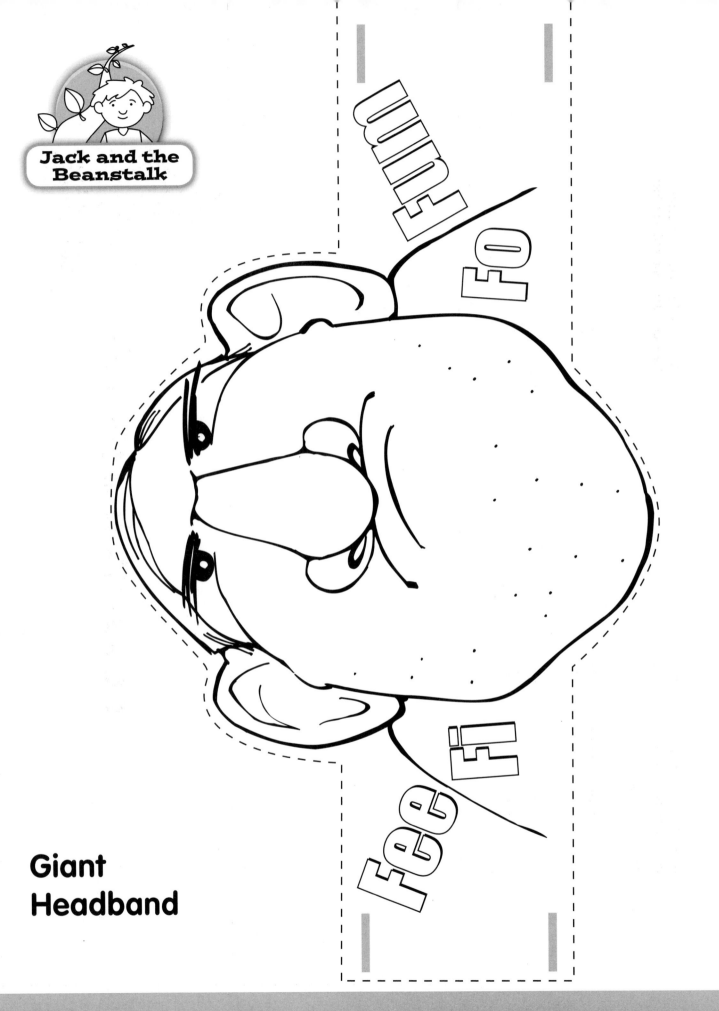

Jack and the Beanstalk

Fee Fi Fo Fum

Giant
Headband

1 Cut out the three pieces of the headband.
Cut along the dashed lines.

2 Staple the pieces together.

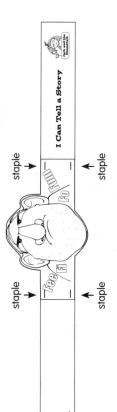

staple →

← staple

I Can Tell a Story

staple →

← staple

3 Fit the band around the student's head and staple the ends together.

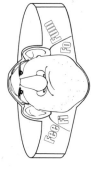

I Can Tell a Story

Jack and the Beanstalk

Chicken Licken

A little chick convinces other barnyard birds
that the sky is falling.

Handouts

Reproduce for each student.

- Meet the Characters
  Page 141
- Follow the Story
  Page 142

Headbands

Make a headband pattern for each student.

- Chicken Licken
  Pages 144 and 145
- Henny Penny
  Pages 146 and 147
- Turkey Lurkey
  Pages 148 and 149
- Ducky Lucky
  Pages 150 and 151
- Foxy Woxy
  Pages 152 and 153

1 Build Background

Distribute page 141 and tell students they will be hearing a make-believe story about a little chick who thinks the sky is falling. Say that all the other barnyard birds (name them) believe the chick and start to panic.

Guide students through the activities on the page. Then share some relevant facts about the characters, such as that foxes eat birds and, for some people, hunting foxes is a sport. You may also want to show a picture of an acorn, or let students handle a real acorn. Explain that acorns are seeds that fall from oak trees. Tell students they will be hearing a story about something that happens because of a falling acorn.

2 Read *Chicken Licken*

Read the story aloud. Show students the illustrations as you read. Act frightened when the birds panic, and invite students to join in each time you read "The sky is falling! The sky is falling!"

3 Reread the Story

Distribute page 142. Tell students to look at the pictures on the page as you reread the story. The pictures are arranged and numbered in story sequence. When you come to an illustration in the story, have the students find the picture on the sheet that shows what you are reading about. Ask them to point to the picture. You may also want to ask them to tell you the number of the picture. Explain how the numbers can help them follow the story.

4 Talk About the Story

Have the students color the pictures on page 142. Encourage them to talk about what's happening in the pictures as they work.

5 Make Headbands

Give each student a headband pattern to color, cut out, and assemble. You may want to have the students work in groups, with each group making headbands for a particular character. Invite students to wear their headbands as you read the story again. Encourage them to pantomime the actions of their headband's character. You may also want to have students wearing Henny Penny, Turkey Lurkey, and Ducky Lucky headbands repeat the sound their character makes when it is frightened.

6 Read Other Versions

Gather other versions of *Chicken Licken* to read to the students. Some versions are titled *Henny Penny* or *Chicken Little*. Lead students in comparing and contrasting the different versions.

7 Assign Roles and Practice Actions

Choose a very energetic student to play Chicken Licken. A student with lots of confidence may be the best choice for sly Foxy Woxy. Ask for a volunteer to drop the acorn to start the story. If you use a real acorn, demonstrate how to drop it without actually hitting anyone.

Have students look at their "Follow the Story" pictures as you review the story's main events with them. Invite students to suggest ways to act out these events. Then give them time to practice their actions. One way to act out the running in the story is to have Chicken Licken move from chair to chair as each of the other birds joins the action. Starting near Henny Penny, who is farthest from Foxy Woxy's den, Chicken Licken will move next to Turkey Lurkey, then to Ducky Lucky, and will end up next to Foxy Woxy's den.

8 Set Up Scenery and Props

Set up a row of four chairs, one for each of the barnyard birds. For Foxy Woxy's den, place a table with a blanket over it at one end of the row of chairs and hang a sign on it *(see page 140)*.

9 Retell the Story

Invite students to wear their headbands and retell the story in their own words. For each group of storytellers, introduce the story and its setting as a signal to begin.

10 Invite an Audience *(optional)*

When students are comfortable retelling the story, you may want to invite an audience to watch them and cheer them on. You will find a reproducible invitation on page 176.

Props
- 4 chairs
- Table covered with a blanket
- "Foxy's den" sign *(see page 140)*
- Real or cardboard acorn

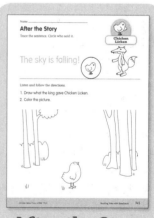

After the Story
Reproduce page 143 for each student. Distribute the copies and help students complete the activities.

Chicken Licken

Once upon a time, Chicken Licken was out in the woods, looking for worms to eat. All of a sudden...*KERPLUNK!* An acorn fell and hit him on the head.

"Help! Help!" cried Chicken Licken. "The sky is falling! The sky is falling!"

The scared little chick ran around and around in circles before he finally found his way out of the woods. He was running so fast that he nearly bumped into Henny Penny.

"My goodness! Where are you going so fast?" asked Henny Penny.

Chicken Licken cheeped, "The sky is falling! The sky is falling! I must warn the king!"

"How do you know the sky is falling?" asked Henny Penny.

"A piece of sky hit me on the head!" said Chicken Licken.

Henny Penny's beak started to shake. She was so frightened that she clucked three times. *Cluck! Cluck! Cluck!* And off they ran to warn the king.

Turkey Lurkey saw Chicken Licken and Henny Penny dash by. "Where are you going so fast?" he called to them.

Chicken Licken cried, "The sky is falling! The sky is falling! We must warn the king!"

"How do you know the sky is falling?" asked Turkey Lurkey.

Henny Penny said, "A piece of sky hit Chicken Licken on the head!"

Turkey Lurkey's tail feathers began to shake. He was so scared that he gobbled three times. *Gobble! Gobble! Gobble!* And they all ran off to warn the king.

As the birds raced past the pond, Ducky Lucky asked, "Where are you going so fast?"

Chicken Licken replied, "The sky is falling! The sky is falling! We must warn the king!"

"How do you know the sky is falling?" asked Ducky Lucky.

Turkey Lurkey said, "A piece of sky hit Chicken Licken on the head!"

Ducky Lucky's eyes began to blinkity blink. She was so scared that she quacked three times. *Quack! Quack! Quack!* And they all ran to warn the king.

The birds ran along until they met Foxy Woxy. "Where are you going?" asked Foxy Woxy.

Chicken Licken answered, "The sky is falling! The sky is falling! We must warn the king!"

Foxy Woxy asked, "How do you know the sky is falling?"

Ducky Lucky said, "A piece of sky hit Chicken Licken on the head!"

"Follow me," said Foxy Woxy. "I will show you the fastest way to get to the king."

EMC 3322 • © Evan-Moor Corp.

Of course, Foxy Woxy was going to lead the birds into his dark den. He thought that four birds would make a delicious dinner, and he was very hungry.

As Chicken Licken, Henny Penny, Turkey Lurkey, and Ducky Lucky started following Foxy Woxy, they heard dogs barking. The king's hunting dogs had smelled the fox. As the dogs chased Foxy Woxy far, far away, the birds ran on to warn the king.

The wise king listened calmly to Chicken Licken's story. Then the king gave Chicken Licken an umbrella.

"Hold this umbrella over your head whenever you go into the woods," the king said.

Now if an acorn falls *KERPLUNK!*, Chicken Licken will not feel a thing.

Foxy's den

1 Reproduce and cut along dashed lines.

2 Fold in half along center line.

Name _____

Meet the Characters

Trace the names. Match the picture and the name.

-  Chicken Licken

-  Henny Penny

-  Turkey Lurkey

-  Ducky Lucky

- Foxy Woxy

Read and circle the answer.

I am a bird.   I live in a den.

Name _____

Follow the Story

Chicken Licken

1

2

3

4

5

Name _____

After the Story

Trace the sentence. Circle who said it.

Chicken Licken

The sky is falling!

Listen and follow the directions.

1. Draw what the king gave Chicken Licken.

2. Color the picture.

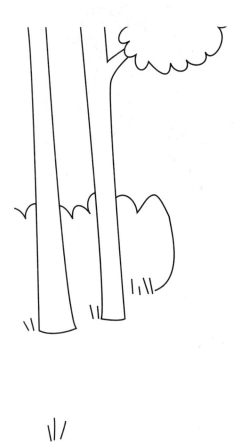

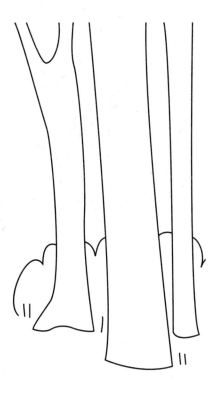

Chicken Licken
Headband

1. Cut out the three pieces of the headband.
   Cut along the dashed lines.
2. Staple the pieces together.

staple → ← staple

staple → ← staple

I Can Tell a Story

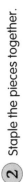

3. Fit the band around the student's head and staple the ends together.

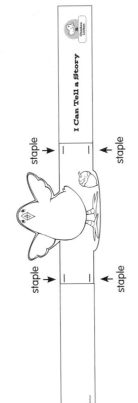

© Evan-Moor Corp. • EMC 3322

I Can Tell a Story

Chicken Licken

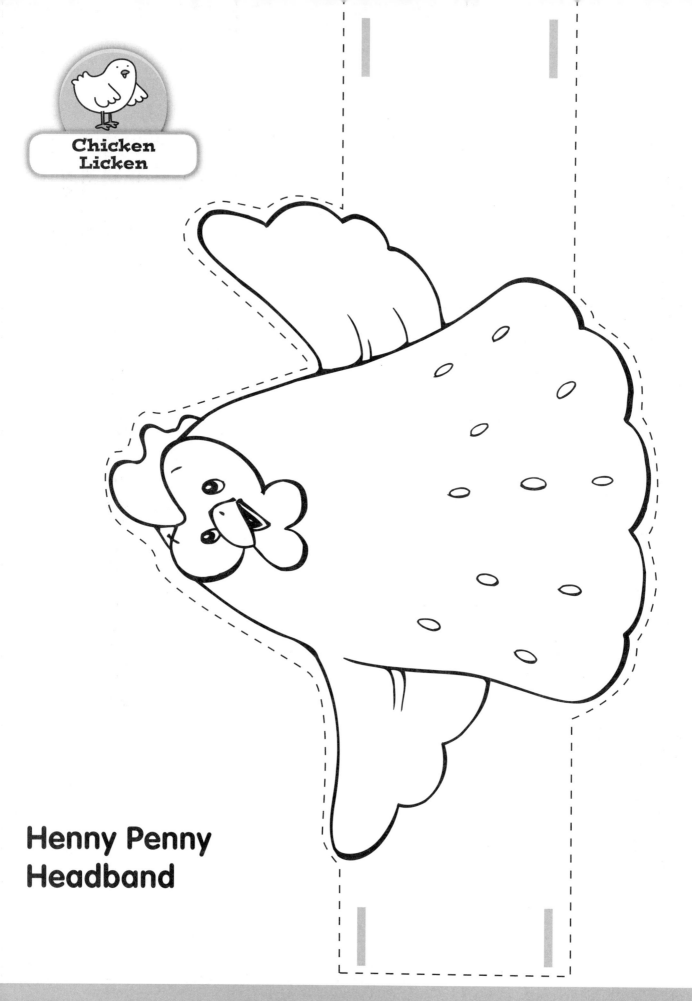

Chicken Licken

Henny Penny Headband

1 Cut out the three pieces of the headband. Cut along the dashed lines.

2 Staple the pieces together.

3 Fit the band around the student's head and staple the ends together.

staple → I Can Tell a Story ← staple

staple → ← staple

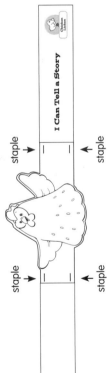

I Can Tell a Story

Chicken
Licken

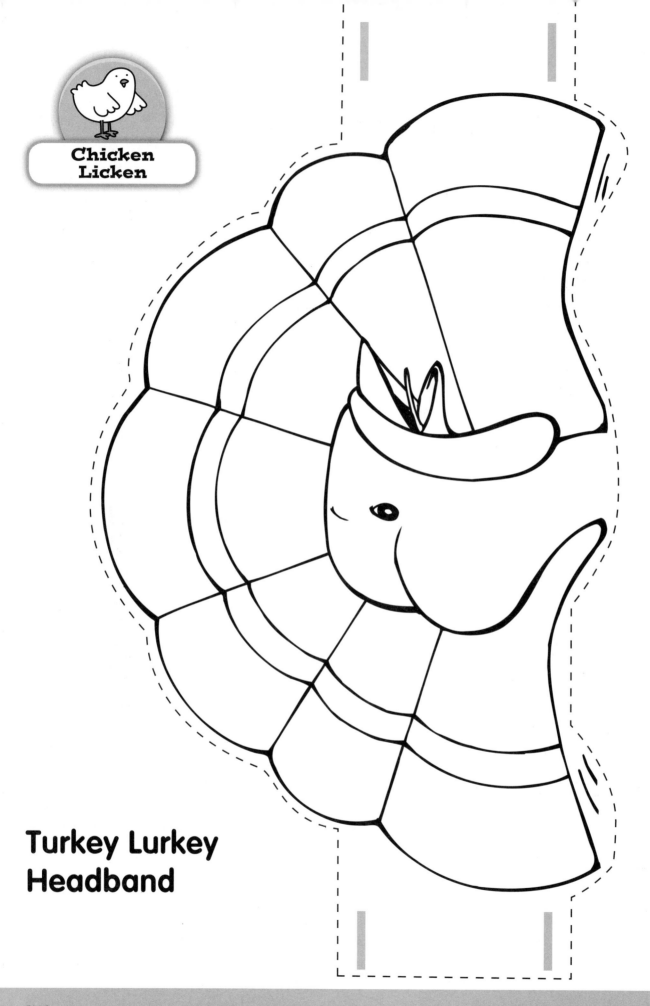

**Turkey Lurkey
Headband**

1 Cut out the three pieces of the headband.
Cut along the dashed lines.

2 Staple the pieces together.

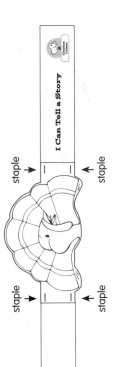

staple → ← staple

staple → ← staple

I Can Tell a Story

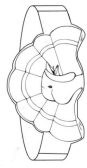

3 Fit the band around the student's head and staple the ends together.

I Can Tell a Story

Chicken Licken

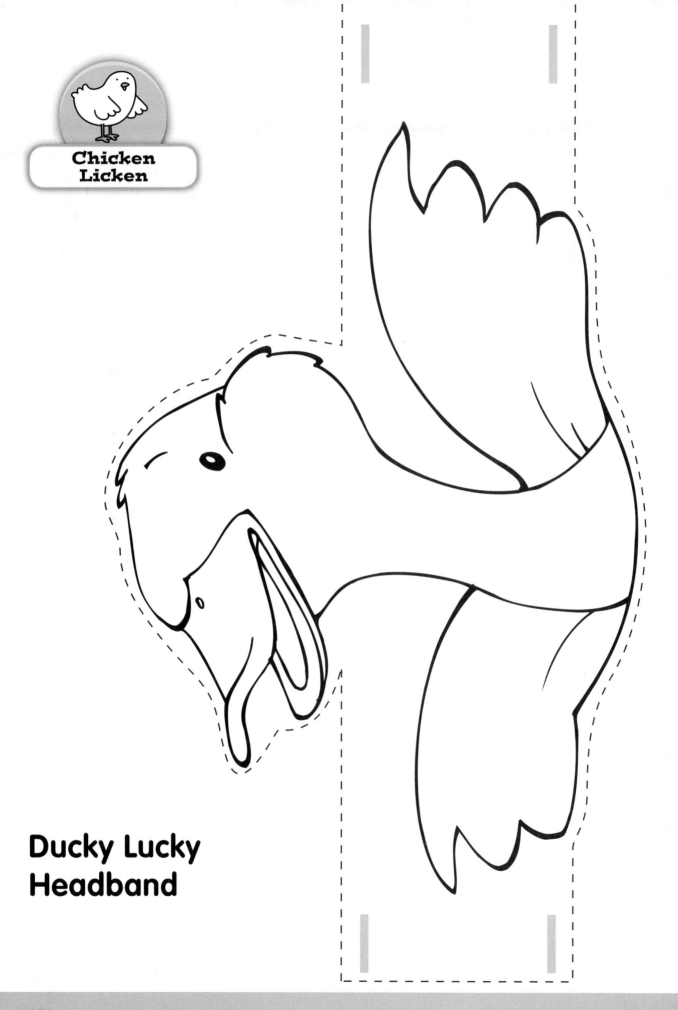

Chicken
Licken

**Ducky Lucky
Headband**

1 Cut out the three pieces of the headband. Cut along the dashed lines.

2 Staple the pieces together.

3 Fit the band around the student's head and staple the ends together.

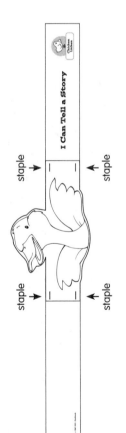

staple → I Can Tell a Story

staple →

staple →

staple →

I Can Tell a Story

Chicken Licken

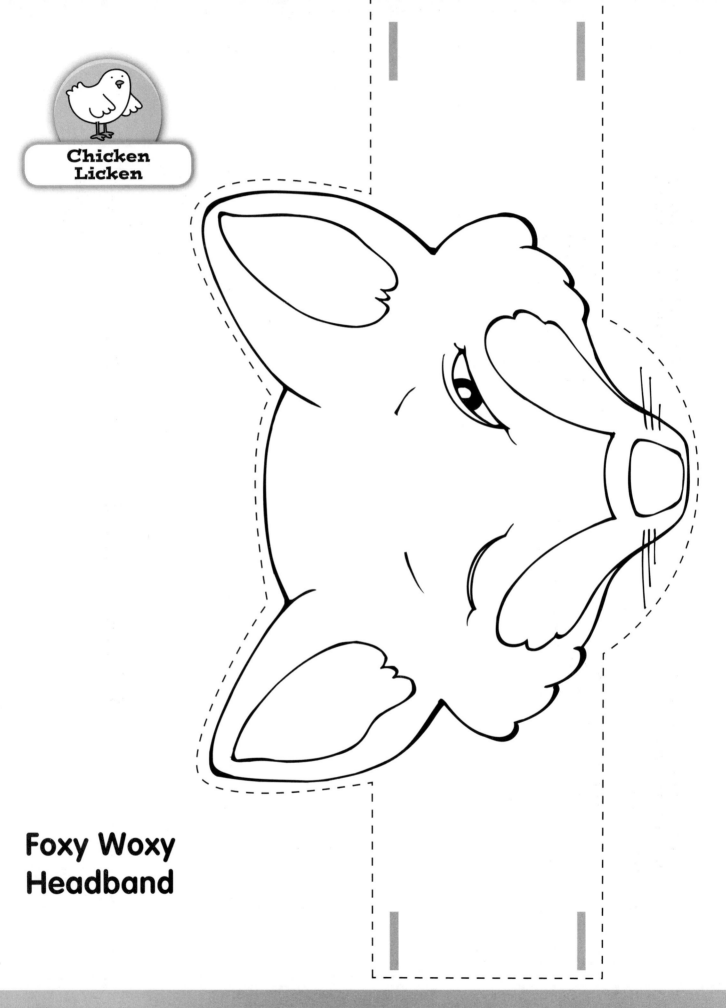

**Chicken
Licken**

Foxy Woxy
Headband

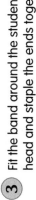

1 Cut out the three pieces of the headband.
Cut along the dashed lines.

2 Staple the pieces together.

3 Fit the band around the student's head and staple the ends together.

staple →

staple →

→ staple

→ staple

I Can Tell a Story

I Can Tell a Story

Chicken Licken

The Gingerbread Man

*A gingerbread man escapes from the oven and runs
away from everyone, except a clever fox.*

Handouts
*Reproduce for each
student.*

- Meet the
  Characters
  Page 161
- Follow the Story
  Page 162

Headbands
*Make a headband
pattern for each
student.*

- Gingerbread Man
  Pages 164 and 165
- Old Woman
  Pages 166 and 167
- Horse
  Pages 168 and 169
- Cow
  Pages 170 and 171
- Sheep
  Pages 172 and 173
- Fox
  Pages 174 and 175

1 Build Background

Distribute page 161 and tell students they will be hearing a make-believe
story about a gingerbread cookie that comes to life and runs away. Have
students point to each picture on the page as you name the character and
tell them a simple fact about the character that helps reveal the storyline,
such as that the old woman is the person who made the gingerbread cookie.

Guide students through the activities on the page. Then invite students to
share cookie-making experiences they have had.

2 Read *The Gingerbread Man*

Read the story aloud. Show students the illustrations as you read. You
may want to help the students learn the gingerbread man's rhyme and
then encourage them to join you in saying or singing the rhyme as you
read the story.

3 Reread the Story

Distribute page 162. Tell students to look at the pictures on the page as you
reread the story. The pictures are arranged and numbered in story sequence.
When you come to an illustration in the story, have the students find the
picture on the sheet that shows what you are reading about. Ask them to
point to the picture. You may also want to ask them to tell you the number
of the picture. Explain how the numbers can help them follow the story.

4 Talk About the Story

Have the students color the pictures on page 162. Encourage them to talk
about what's happening in the pictures as they work.

5 Make Headbands

Give each student a headband pattern to color, cut out, and assemble.
You may want to have the students work in groups, with each group
making headbands for a particular character. Invite students to wear their
headbands as you read the story again. Encourage them to pantomime
the actions of their headband's character, and ask all students to say or
sing the gingerbread man's rhyme.

6 Read Other Versions

Gather other versions of *The Gingerbread Man* or *The Gingerbread Boy* to
read to the students, and then lead them in comparing and contrasting
the different versions.

7. Assign Roles and Practice Actions

For the role of the gingerbread man, choose a lively student who will say or sing the rhymes gleefully. Students who tend to be shy or have trouble remembering the words may prefer to be in a chorus. You could have the gingerbread man say or sing his rhymes with the chorus or simply pantomime the actions. For the role of the fox, choose a student who is good at acting sly or mischievous.

Have students look at their "Follow the Story" pictures as you review the story's main events with them. Invite students to suggest ways to act out these events. Then give them time to practice their actions. For the chase scenes, the characters could either run around a row of chairs, or the old woman and the gingerbread man could simply move from chair to chair as each animal joins the chase. For the river scene, have the fox stand and hold the river sign *(see page 160)*, while the gingerbread man slowly ducks down below it.

8. Set Up Scenery and Props

Arrange four chairs in a single row. Have the fox stand slightly off to the right, holding the river sign. You may want to reproduce the river sign on blue paper, or you could just color it blue.

9. Retell the Story

Invite students to wear their headbands and retell the story in their own words. For each group of storytellers, introduce the story and its setting as a signal to begin.

10. Invite an Audience *(optional)*

When students are comfortable retelling the story, you may want to invite an audience to watch them and cheer them on. You will find a reproducible invitation on page 176.

Props
- 4 chairs
- "River" sign *(see page 160)*

After the Story
Reproduce page 163 for each student. Distribute the copies and help students complete the activities.

The Gingerbread Man

One crisp fall day, an old woman decided to bake a gingerbread cookie. She shaped the dough until it looked like a little man. She gave the man raisin eyes, a chocolate chip nose, and a smile made of round red cinnamon candies. Then she popped the gingerbread man into the oven to bake.

When the cookie was ready, the old woman opened the oven door and pulled out the pan. "Ahhh, you smell good!" she said.

To the woman's great surprise, the gingerbread man jumped off the pan and ran out the door as fast as he could go!

The old woman chased the gingerbread man, but she could not catch him. "Stop!" she said. "I want to eat you!"

The gingerbread man just laughed and sang,

Run, run, as fast as you can!
You can't catch me!
I'm the gingerbread man!

The gingerbread man did not stop running. As he passed a horse, the horse called out, "Stop, gingerbread man! I want to eat you!"

The gingerbread man ran on and sang,

Run, run, as fast as you can!
You can't catch me!
I'm the gingerbread man!

Now the horse and the old woman were both chasing the gingerbread man, but they could not catch him.

The gingerbread man ran on and on. As he passed a cow, the cow said, "Stop, gingerbread man! I want to eat you!"

The gingerbread man did not stop. He just ran and sang,

Run, run, as fast as you can!
You can't catch me!
I'm the gingerbread man!

Now the cow led the chase, with the horse and the old woman close behind. They all chased the gingerbread man, but they could not catch him.

When the gingerbread man passed a sheep, the sheep said, "Stop, gingerbread man! I want to eat you!"

Of course, the little gingerbread man kept running and singing,

> *Run, run, as fast as you can!*
> *You can't catch me!*
> *I'm the gingerbread man!*

And so the sheep joined the chase, with the cow, the horse, and the old woman close behind. They all ran as fast as they could, but not one of them could catch the gingerbread man!

The little gingerbread man just ran and ran. As he ran past a fox, he sang,

> *Run, run, as fast as you can!*
> *You can't catch me!*
> *I'm the gingerbread man!*

The fox ran after him, too, until they came to a river. There, the little gingerbread man stopped running. He could not swim!

The sly fox smiled and said, "I don't want to eat you. I want to help you get away. Jump on my tail. I will take you across the river."

The gingerbread man looked at the fox. The fox had big, sharp teeth! He watched the fox slip into the river.

"I really want to get away," said the gingerbread man. "Wait for me to jump onto your tail."

When they were halfway across the river, the fox smiled again. And with a quick flick of his tail, he flipped the gingerbread man into the air. As the little cookie tumbled downward, the hungry fox opened its mouth and...

GULP!

"That was a yummy snack!" said the fox.

Retelling Tales with Headbands

Reproduce and cut along dashed lines.

Name _____

Meet the Characters

Trace the names. Match the picture and the name.

 • old woman

• gingerbread man

 • horse

• cow

• sheep

• fox

Read and circle the answer.

I baked a cookie.

Name _____

Follow the Story

①

②

③

④

⑤

Retelling Tales with Headbands   EMC 3322 • © Evan-Moor Corp.

Name _____

After the Story

Trace the sentence. Circle who said it.

You can't catch me!

Listen and follow the directions.

1. Draw the gingerbread man running.

2. Color the picture.

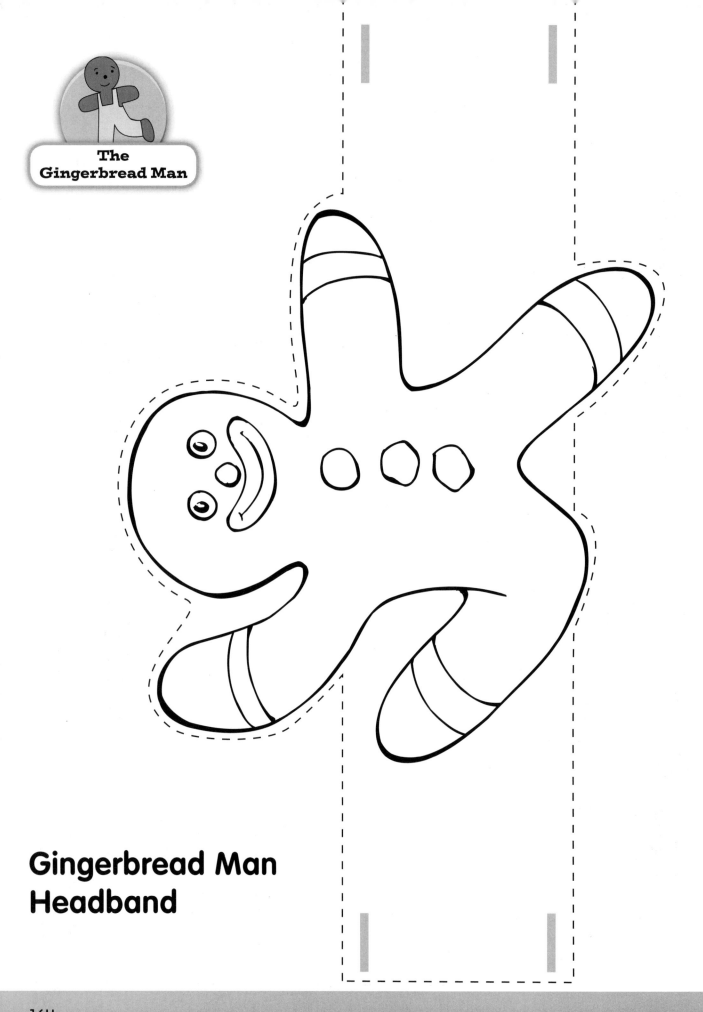

The Gingerbread Man

Gingerbread Man Headband

1 Cut out the three pieces of the headband.
Cut along the dashed lines.

2 Staple the pieces together.

3 Fit the band around the student's head and staple the ends together.

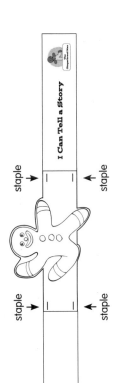

staple →

staple →

← staple

← staple

I Can Tell a Story

I Can Tell a Story

The Gingerbread Man

**Old Woman
Headband**

1 Cut out the three pieces of the headband. Cut along the dashed lines.

2 Staple the pieces together.

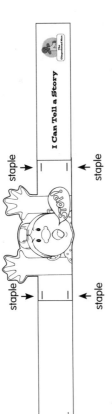

staple

staple

I Can Tell a Story

staple

staple

3 Fit the band around the student's head and staple the ends together.

I Can Tell a Story

The Gingerbread Man

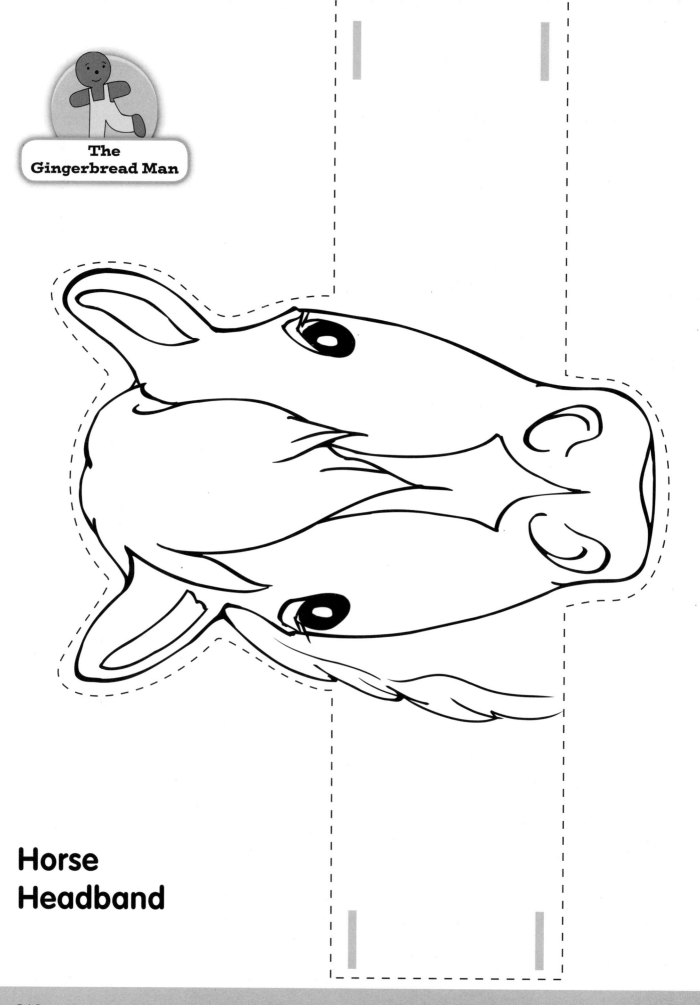

Horse
Headband

1 Cut out the three pieces of the headband.
Cut along the dashed lines.

2 Staple the pieces together.

3 Fit the band around the student's head and staple the ends together.

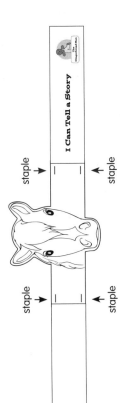

staple → ← staple

I Can Tell a Story

staple → ← staple

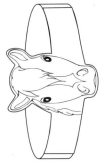

I Can Tell a Story

The Gingerbread Man

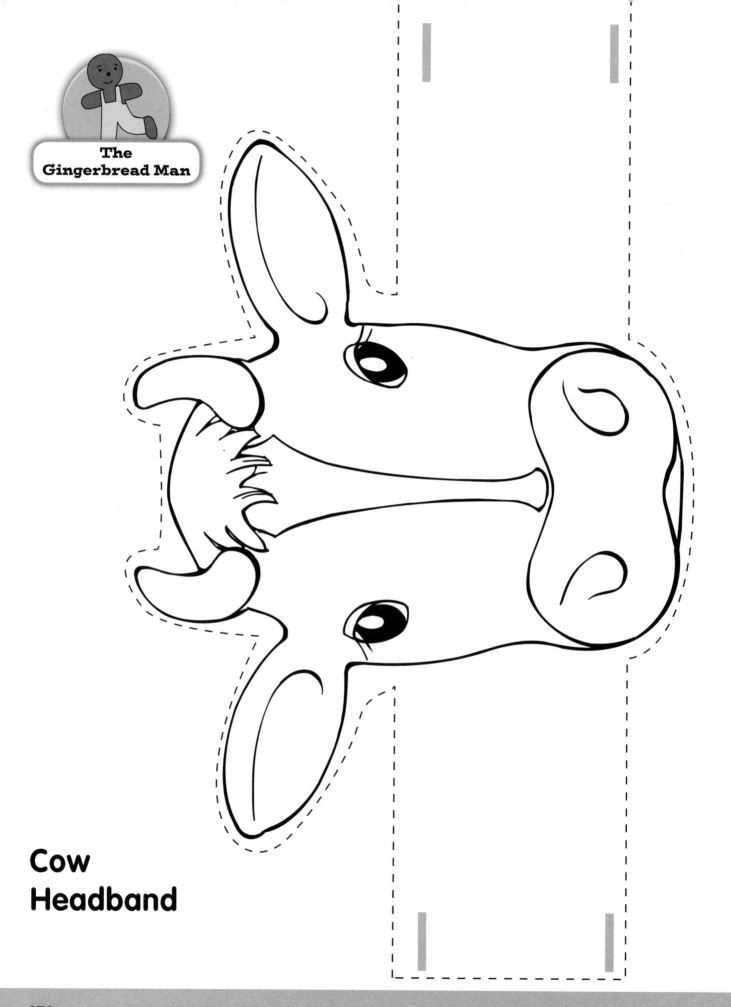

Cow
Headband

1 Cut out the three pieces of the headband.
Cut along the dashed lines.

2 Staple the pieces together.

3 Fit the band around the student's head and staple the ends together.

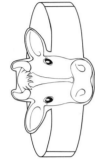

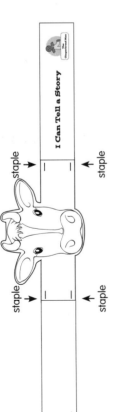

I Can Tell a Story

staple → ← staple

staple → ← staple

I Can Tell a Story

The
Gingerbread Man

Retelling Tales with Headbands   **171**

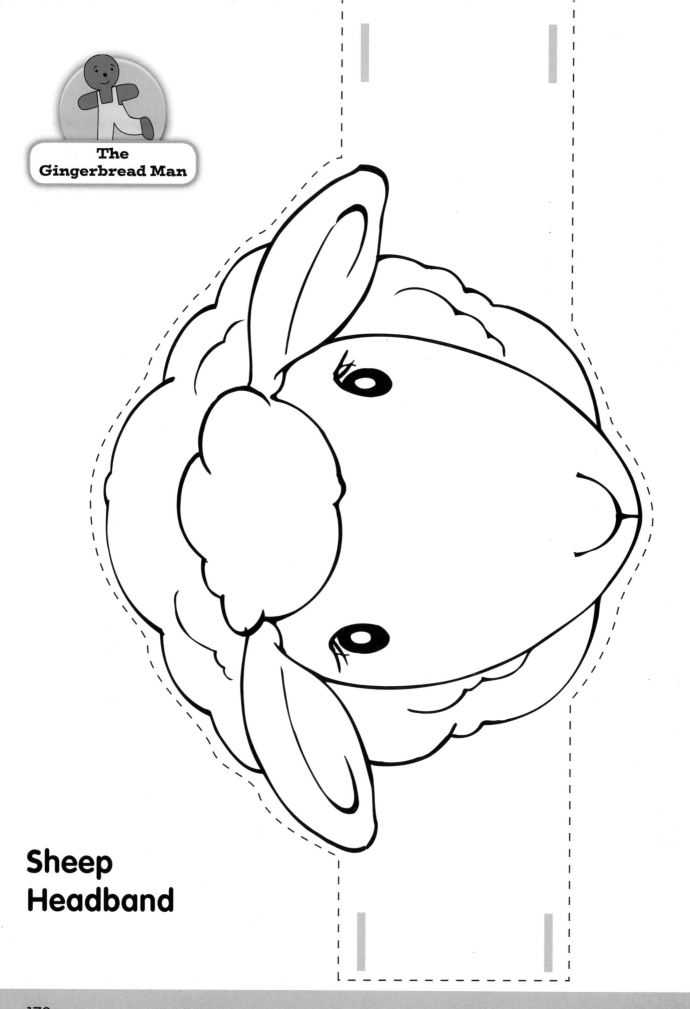

Sheep
Headband

1 Cut out the three pieces of the headband. Cut along the dashed lines.

2 Staple the pieces together.

3 Fit the band around the student's head and staple the ends together.

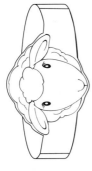

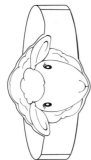

staple →
→ staple
staple →
→ staple

I Can Tell a Story

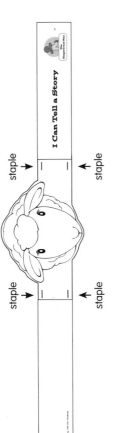

I Can Tell a Story

The Gingerbread Man

© Evan-Moor Corp. • EMC 3322

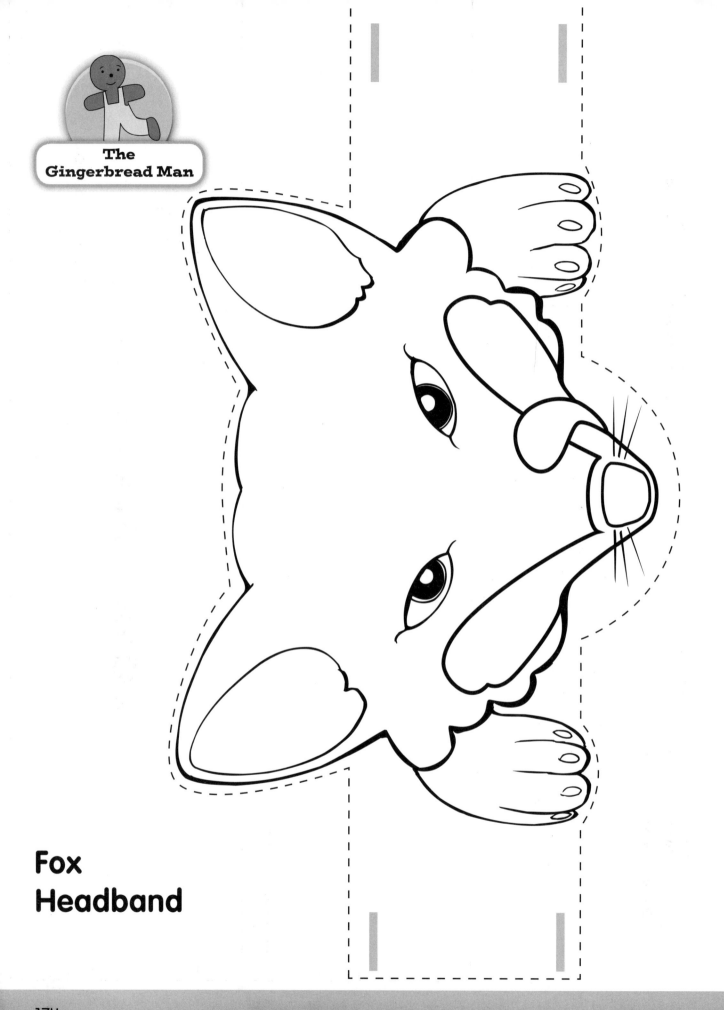

Fox
Headband

1 Cut out the three pieces of the headband.
Cut along the dashed lines.

2 Staple the pieces together.

staple → ← staple

staple → ← staple

I Can Tell a Story

3 Fit the band around the student's
head and staple the ends together.

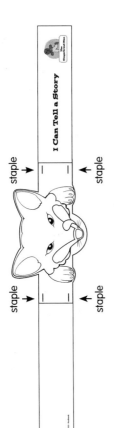

I Can Tell a Story

The
Gingerbread Man

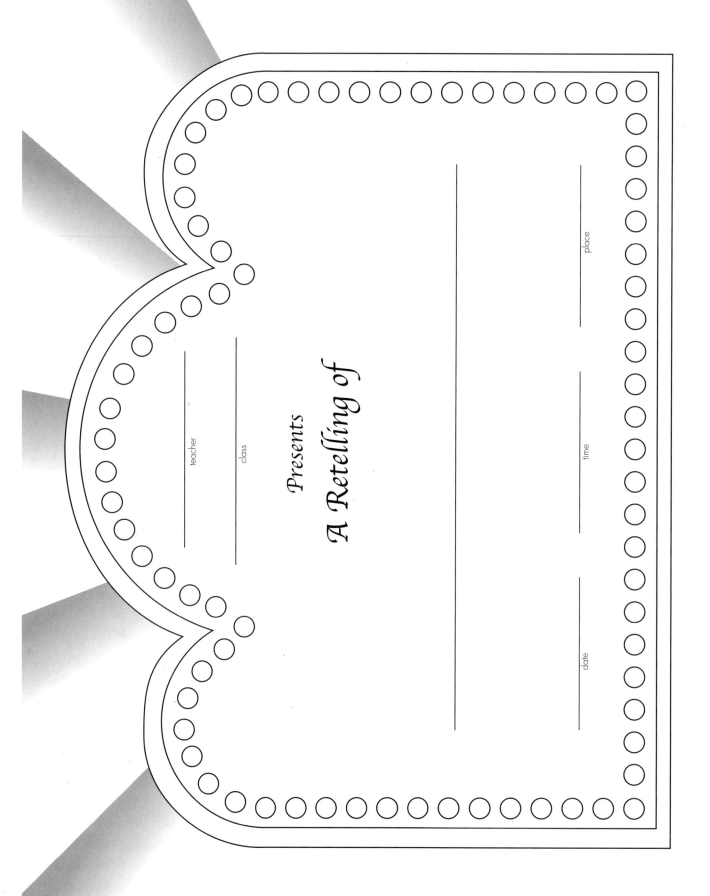

Presents

A Retelling of

teacher

class

place

time

date